A Dry
and
Thirsty
Ground

A Dry and Thirsty Ground

MIKE WEISS

ST. MARTIN'S PRESS
NEW YORK

Library of Congress Cataloging-in-Publication Data

Weiss, Mike.
    A dry and thirsty ground / Mike Weiss.
        p.   cm.
    "A Thomas Dunne book."
    ISBN 0-312-06956-1
  I. Title.
  PS3573.E4162D7   1992
  813'.54—dc20   91-41106
                                                          CIP

First Edition: April 1992
10 9 8 7 6 5 4 3 2 1

My girls: Rhoda, Carole, Bess, and Casey. And in memory of Shirley Hersch, 1900–1989.

"But she was plucked up in a fury, she was cast down to the ground, and the east wind dried up her fruit: her strong rods were broken and withered; the fire consumed them.

"And now she is planted in the wilderness, in a dry and thirsty ground."

Ezekiel, XIX, 12, 13

A Dry
and
Thirsty
Ground

One

The razor was at my throat. I was afraid to so much as sigh, and concentrated on keeping my breathing shallow. I was trussed up and tilted back in the chair, the captive of the silent, silver-haired Italian, his straight-edge razor delicately but firmly pressed beneath my jaw. Slowly, he pulled the razor across my skin as far as my chin, and my Adam's apple bobbed like some silly cartoon.

He wiped the razor clean on a towel and stropped it loudly. This agony, believe it or not, was a kind of celebration: a little something for myself while I was still on the full-court side of forty. I had reached the end of that sadly neglected American festival, the close of the fiscal year, with a comfortably larger pile of chips than I had brought to the table, and a barbershop shave, my first, was a way of being good to myself. You live in California long enough, believe me, you start to think this way.

The silent Italian began a second stroke, this one brushing the edge of my jumpy Adam's apple. Jesus, Mary, and Joseph. The hot towels covering my face, thank God, hid the fact that my eyes were squeezed shut. The thought that he would soon begin scraping beneath my nose—an area of utmost sensitivity that required great delicacy and finesse to avoid nicks when I worked the edge of the old Gillette in front of my bathroom mirror—was almost too much to bear.

What made his razor so frightening was not just the threatening feel of its treacherous edge against my only breathing apparatus, but his complete ignorance of my face. In a million years I couldn't convey to him all I knew about shaving my own face. How could I ever explain that he needed to put precisely enough pressure on the razor when he reached the cleft between my underlip and chin where the stubble was prickly but the skin soft? These were the things you could never explain to anyone else, this knowledge of the hand.

When the silent Italian was finally done with me after, oh, forty or fifty years in his chair, there was a sore spot at the left corner of my mouth, another beneath my left ear, and a third on my throat that I knew would sting for days. My face felt raw and naked.

As I released myself from his chair I slowly became aware again of my surroundings: the talc and witch hazel smell of the hotel shop, the snick of shears, the Muzak, the barber's hairy wrist and knuckles extending from the sleeve of his white smock, offering my change, which I waved away. I all but fled.

My telephone was ringing so I darted up the steps two at a time, all twenty-seven of them, fumbled with the key, and made it through the door just as the phone went silent in midring. I picked it up anyway and heard Peter saying, in his formal, Belgian manner, "You have reached Mr. Be-en Henry." A familiar voice I couldn't quite place replied, "Oh Christ, where is he?"

"Peter," I interrupted, "I'm on."

"Oh good," he said, and clicked off.

"Bunko? It's Paul."

"I know, Paulie, nobody else calls me Bunko anymore."

"Estelle does once in awhile," he said, with his passion for accuracy. "Bunko, I'm in trouble." He was, too, I could hear that much.

"What's wrong?"

"I'm in jail."

"Where?" I picked up a pencil.

"Monterey County Adult Detention Center," he said.

Another voice I could hear but not make out said something and then Paulie added, "In Salinas, on Natividad Road."

"Good, that's close, I can be there in a couple of hours, but what—"

"Murder."

I didn't know what to say. There was a silence on the line.

"I can see why they'd suspect you," I finally told my oldest friend, my coconspirator in surviving adolescence, "you've got a long history of jaywalking."

He couldn't manage a laugh and I didn't blame him. It wasn't funny. "What have you done about a lawyer?" I asked him.

"Well, nothing really; there's this guy in Carmel Valley, I could use him I guess—he handled it when I bought my place, and—"

"Look," I cut in, "let me handle the lawyer. I'll get someone good. I'll be down later tonight, we can talk more then."

"I don't know if they allow visitors or anything."

"I'm not a visitor, I'm your investigator. Tell the guard there I'm coming, that you've engaged Jacob Braunstein of San Francisco as your attorney, and that I'm on my way down there on his behalf. And don't worry if he gives you a song and dance, legally they have to let me in."

"I'm glad you're coming, Bunko," Paulie said.

"Me too." I touched the sore spot at the corner of my mouth with a fingertip.

Two

Braunstein was in court on a motion to suppress when I called the office, but Giselle told me he'd be back any minute so I packed an overnight bag, let Peter know I'd be out of town, and left him Paulie's number down near Big Sur. By the time Braunstein finally rang back I was sweeping the kitchen for the second time to keep from climbing the walls, and there wasn't a speck of dust to be found on any surface in Chez Henry.

"Brother Henry," he began, sounding as if he were speaking through a megaphone at the bottom of the Grand Canyon.

"Jake, get off the goddamn power phone or I'll rip you a new mouth."

"That better?"

"Why the hell do you use that thing? It sounds like the bogeyman in a second-rate nightmare."

"Son," said Braunstein, who was at least five years younger than I was, "you've never understood the necessity of appearances. You have to let the people know you have what they think they want, and that makes them want you. A man cannot survive by talent, charm, and looks alone, not in my bracket. So, *nu?* Our young friend Pilcher hasn't vamoosed, has he?"

At the moment I was babysitting a material witness to a double homicide that Braunstein was handling in Redwood City, a scared, strung out crackhead I had tracked to Seattle and brought home by the ear. I didn't like to work for lawyers, but at least Braunstein had never bargained over my fee, and though that was in his favor it wasn't why I could work for him. I knew Braunstein's story and he knew I knew it. Working for anybody else is always a mistake unless you have some leverage of your own; in the absence of a trade union for people in my line of work, knowledge had to suffice.

When I had first met Jake Braunstein he was taking the excursion route through law school, dealing grass, and keeping a pet python in a hollowed-out television set. He drove an ancient MGB, spent a lot of time in front of a mirror styling his prematurely gray hair, read both the *New York Review of Books* and *Penthouse* from fore to aft in a manner of speaking, and invited girls back to his place to see his pet snake.

Then he met Patricia Reilly Burns. If Patricia, who had been educated by the Sisters of the Sacred Heart, had not happened along and fallen inexplicably in love with the thoroughly disreputable Braunstein, he might well still be keeping company with the snake while living just around the corner from the law and the cops both. When Patricia had been around long enough for Braunstein to become besotted with satisfaction and mad with longing, she made it clear what steps had to be taken in order to keep her.

Braunstein stopped dealing. He completed his course at Boalt Hall with honors. After they married Patricia let him keep the python until she became pregnant with their first child. Now he drove from their home in Tiburon in a big-ass Mercedes that burned high-acceleration retainers in its tank. And every time another woebegone dealer paid Braunstein an outrageous fee to keep his sorry ass out of prison, Patricia Reilly Burns Braunstein's husband brought home three-dozen American beauty roses. It was a Jew's devotional offering.

"Pilcher'll stay put, Jake, or if not I'll go get him again. This is something else." I explained what little I knew about Paulie's trouble, and enough about my relationships with Estelle, Paulie's mother, and Paulie himself so that Braunstein would understand I was talking family.

He agreed to fly down first thing in the morning in his little Cessna.

"What about posting bail, what are his circumstances?" Ever since the feds had begun to enforce the forfeiture statute the fees of criminal lawyers had become somewhat more problematical, and though there wasn't a greedy man among them they were a prudent lot.

"You know those collections of old baseball cards and comic books and stamps and stuff that guys are always moaning that their mothers threw out, Jake? Paul's mom, Estelle, saved everything. She had a feeling, you know? And his dad worked for the Cubs, so all the baseball cards were autographed. Last year he cashed out."

"Ahh," said Braunstein, making a sound as expensive as the sibilance of silk against silk. "Not that it matters, of course. Not if he's practically your brother."

I tuned the car radio into a station broadcasting Newzak—the coinage, alas, wasn't mine but Malcolm Muggeridge's—to hear if the copter jockette had spotted any problems along the route I planned to take out of town. It was killer-rush hour and the freeways were clogged.

I slid out of North Beach by the back door, over the hill and down to the Embarcadero. As I ran along the waterfront near the Bay Bridge the radio said four thousand firefighters were battling the Lost Sam fire in Los Padres National Forest. I hadn't connected the fire, which had been burning for several days, to Paulie but now it clicked. Scottsburg, where Paul had bought a home, was at the edge of Los Padres, if I wasn't mistaken. When I stopped for gas I pulled out my road atlas to check the geography. I was studying the map when an attendant came up to my open window.

"Fill it?"

"Yeah, high test," I said absently. When I looked up he hadn't budged.

"I don't understand," he admitted. "What kind of gas you want?" He was about seventeen. I felt my age.

"Premium, son," I told him. Scottsburg looked to be inside Los Padres.

The informed impulse of an old cabdriver was still in working order, and the traffic south on 280 where I picked it up off Mariposa was blithe sailing. The black Seville rolled along smoothly at seventy. I switched to KJAZ and my mind went on cruise control cocooned by burgundy leather. My cigars and two take-out coffees were at the ready and I was soon roadborne. Memories of Paulie segued into the consideration of profane acts, thoughts of Jessica Gage, momentary road awareness, more profane acts past and fantastical, and then a fragmentary but densely detailed recollection of the twenty-seven-inning stickball game Paulie and I had played the night my ma died. The memory came complete with the smell of hot asphalt cooling in the evening shadows, the sounds of television heard through open windows, and the bottomless emptiness in the pit of my stomach.

My father had gone years earlier, and it was Paul's mother Estelle Richards who had opened her heart and her spare room to me. Estelle was big-hearted but not exactly easygoing. Then again, having a frightened, angry, and defiant sixteen-year old as a permanent houseguest hadn't exactly been a bowl of strawberries and cream itself. Estelle and Paul were the closest thing I had to family.

It had been about a year since Paul had fetched up unexpectedly near Big Sur, on leave from Harcourt Brace Jovanovich, and living in the woods. Now that I thought of it, it was out of character for Paul not to have invited me down to his new place. He had been up to see me a couple of times, in fact in May we had seen the Cubbies play the Giants at Candlestick. Box seats in section 4. I had paid a scalper twice their face value because down low along the third baseline I could see into the Giants dugout and try to steal Roger Craig's signs.

I had had the sense that day that something important was happening with Paulie. He hadn't really explained why he had moved so dramatically, not any more than to say he was ready for a change. I hadn't questioned him, figuring that when he wanted to he would tell me. Really we were more like brothers than friends. Estelle seemed to know that something important was changing inside of Paul. She had written and called me more often than usual, always asking if I had talked lately with Paul.

South of San Jose not only the city but the suburbs fell away quickly as I descended into the Salinas Valley. Gilroy flashed by, a stretch of roadside self-storage warehouses and used car dealerships brightened by billboards importuning the passing motorist to eat garlic. KJAZ faded into static. The hills broke up signals and stations came and went. An angry young woman talked about the Cuban people, calling them Koo-ban, and the junta in the country of Chee-lay. Then a nasal professorial woman had a chance only to say, ". . . herpes, syphilis, and viral papilloma," before she was replaced by a male basso profundo: "Built for the human race."

California has got to be America's lost and found. The things I had lost in California were the things people usually lost. San Francisco's version of Ellis Island was divorce court, and I had been processed through and stamped "Alone." Next, I had unexpectedly lost my chosen line of work as a reporter, and then I began to be less certain about the past. What I mean is things that I had once believed defined me came to seem less consequential over time.

I had been satisfied as a reporter for the *Courier* until one day I had offended the wrong people and found myself driving a taxi. *There* was something I worried would define me, but one thing had led to another and now the state of California in its wisdom had licensed me to work as a private investigator. In other words, I was given leave by the government to do what I had always done, ask questions. California was like a

Pacific rim guru smiling enigmatically as it pocketed my fee. The state motto should have been, Are you sure?

Licensed question-asking had turned out to be more profitable than I had imagined. I could make as much money as I wanted, depending on how much I wanted to work. When I was working I was as hard to call off as a Mexican street dog with a juicy bone, but when I could possibly avoid it I didn't work. Any life that precluded a midmorning cappuccino and the sports section in a cafe with enough natural light for reading was a life not worth enduring. There is a certain kind of North Beach cafe where people leave their newspapers behind and the corner table is occupied by old men speaking Italian who make the young girls serving them espressos laugh.

What I found in California wasn't exactly news either. I liked the restlessness and the indifference. Everybody was strictly on his own, which was why there was so much babble about community; in fact I once heard the mayor refer to junkies as the IV community. I was happy with the sense of disbelonging, perhaps because I could not stay where I had come from and would never find a place to take its place. California would do.

I was listening to weeping Spanish guitars and doing eighty-five across the floor of the valley. The radio picked up snatches of news about the Lost Sam fire. I wondered where the name came from, and whether Paul's house was okay, and if the murder he was accused of had anything to do with the fire. What I knew about forest fires began and ended with Smokey the Bear.

The jail wasn't hard to find, it was part of a low-slung complex of ugly, landscaped county buildings along Natividad Road. The Adult Detention Center was a bunker commanding a rise behind a barbed-wire perimeter.

A black deputy who had a gleaming shaved skull and a sharply creased tan uniform was polishing his star with a cloth when I walked into the reception area. It was 7:48. The wall clock had a red sweep-second hand. I bent at the waist to get my mouth close to the talking space in the security glass and said who I was and who I was there to see. The deputy kept polishing his star, though he did turn his head sideways so I could speak directly into his ear, which was well-formed and lay close to his scalp. He had sergeant's stripes and a mole in his right cheek. The room smelled powerfully of disinfectant and stale cigarettes.

He laid the star down carefully and asked me for identification, which I slid onto a tray he pulled through to his side of the glass barrier. Then he nodded toward a bench behind me. "Few minutes," he said. He walked like a weightlifter.

I paced the checked linoleum along well-worn lines. At 8:03 he returned to his chair and his star. At 8:15 he stood and came around to unlock a heavy cast-iron door under the clock and hold it open for me. I followed him along a corridor of cubicles that were light on designer enhancements, until he left me in a government-issue green chair in an office cubicle that contained only one little personal touch, a plaque reading: STRESS: the confusion created when one's mind overrides the body's basic desire to choke the living shit out of some asshole who desperately needs it.

When the sergeant returned again he said, "I'm going to ask you to submit to a search before you can see the prisoner, investigator. Empty your pockets and stand over there with your legs spread and your hands at your side." His pat-down was as brisk, disinterested, and efficient as everything else about him.

He waited in the doorway while I refilled my pockets and then led me through a barred and locked gate that was opened by another deputy, and into a tiny interview room. The light in the room was shockingly bright because the heavy iron mesh around the two-hundred-watt bulb wasn't about shading illumination, it was about not screwing loose a possible weapon. In the tropical glare I saw two chairs, a scraped metal table, a gold ashtray stolen from McDonalds, and an empty Styrofoam cup on the floor in the corner.

"This door locks from outside," he said. "There's no handle inside. Over there, that's the trouble buzzer. If the inmate gets unruly and wants to kick your ass, you press that. It sets off an alarm in Control One. When you finished, this switch here trips a light, we'll come get you."

Paulie appeared behind the sergeant in the doorway, escorted by another deputy. The red prison jumpsuit was sizes too big for him, and made him appear small and overwhelmed. Our eyes met and held over the sergeant's starched shoulder. The other deputy nodded and Paul stepped into the tiny room, blinking. The sergeant shut the door behind him. It slammed with a ghastly clang.

Three

The tiny room felt jammed to capacity with both of us standing. I sat down. Paulie gripped the back of the other chair with both hands, rocking on the balls of his feet as he spoke.

"Listen, Bunko, the fire was already moving into Spiller Canyon last night. It's too steep in there for them to make a firebreak that'll hold, it could have jumped when the inversion level dropped, it goes mad when the inversion breaks."

"Your house?" I asked, not really understanding either the geography or the rest of it.

"I was packing the stuff it was most important to get out when this . . ." He faltered and held the cuff of his felon's red jumpsuit between two fingers to illustrate what he meant. "I don't know," he said, shaking his head, "it's all still up there and there's nobody to look after it, I wanted to get out . . . you know, the important things. I . . ."

I waited and listened while he blew off pressure. Paulie was about six feet tall and built awkwardly, with a concave chest and long sloping shoulders. His hips and thighs were wide and heavy. His head was perhaps a size larger than scale demanded, with a beaky nose, high cheekbones, and a closely shaved beard. His reddish hair was tightly curled and cut short. His habitual expression mixed shrewdness and humor with kindliness. At the moment he was scowling and tense, frightened and self-protective.

"I could go up to your place when I leave here and take out whatever you'd like, Paulie. We'll talk about it later, okay? Tell me what's going on first." I sounded more calm and rational than I felt; it was painfully unsettling to see Paul like this.

"You're right," he said, easing his grip on the back of the chair. "Got a cigarette?" He exhaled deeply and loudly.

I took out three packs and put them on the table. He began to rip the cellophane off one. Impatience made him clumsy. He had been biting his nails. He fumbled a cigarette out and leaned toward the match I struck.

"You smoking?" I asked.

He began to cough with the first drag, shaking his head. "No," he sputtered as his cheeks reddened.

"I didn't think so, that's why I only brought three packs." Under other circumstances Paul would have smiled or said something in the same vein. Instead he said, "I don't know how to start."

"Who are you supposed to have killed?"

He shook his head vehemently, then said, "An asshole named Rich Hanna."

He stopped. I waited.

"It was my ax. They found my ax in his head." He crossed his arms over his chest and rubbed both shoulders. "On my property. I guess I'm supposed to be an ax murderer. Oh man," he cried out, "I can't believe what's happening to me. When can I get out of here?"

"Tomorrow probably, soon. I take it you thought this Rich Hanna would benefit from being killed?"

He lit a second smoke from the glowing butt of the first. "I hated him," he said, meeting my eye. "I thought he was human scum. I was in my place, the fire had closed to within a couple of miles so I was packing some things, I told you that

13

already, and keeping my sprinkler system going. It was just something I rigged, you know, garden hoses." Paul seemed to look inward as the memory took form in his mind. "Rich was driving his nine for the feds, everybody who can is working for the feds, they're paying for men and machinery. He was running his nine right at a beautiful old oak across the creek. The tree was, I don't know, maybe three hundred, four hundred years old. The right place to make that firebreak was nowhere near that tree and that scumbag knew it, he only wanted to bulldoze that old oak because, you know, it was mine. I went over and told him to stop. He just told me to fuck off, you know? It's a long story, Bunko. I was so goddamn furious I slammed my ax into that oak and went back inside.

"Just a little while later, I don't know, maybe five minutes, some hotshots carried him down to my house. They had found him up in the seat with the ax sticking out of his head. When the sheriff came, I guess a couple of the hotshots had seen Rich and me arguing, he talked to everybody and asked me if it was my ax. Then he arrested me. That was . . . only this morning, I keep thinking it was yesterday. I can't believe what's happening to me. Bunko, what am I going to do? I didn't kill anybody, but I feel guilty because I wanted him dead."

"I understand, Paulie. I'm going to ask you some questions, don't read anything into them. I've got to know everything that happened in order to help you."

"You can get me out?" he asked again.

I told him about Braunstein flying down in the morning. "There'll be an arraignment. You'll plead not guilty and they'll set some bail. Paul, why did you take your ax when you went to warn off Rich Hanna? You were inside packing, right? So you had to go get your ax."

The question sent a jolt into him. I saw the fear and something else reach his eyes. "Rich beat me up a couple of months ago in front of a lot of people," he said flatly. "We were at a bar over in CV, Carmel Valley. I guess I took the ax up there to make sure . . . you know."

"What had you fought about?" I asked, amazed at the stilted professionalism of my question. Paulie had no shield against his feelings in these circumstances, but I had work, blessed work.

"He's a fucking bully," Paul said grimly, pounding a fist rhythmically into a palm. "Nothing really, the jukebox, but that was only an excuse to start a fight. Rich comes from the oldest family in Scottsburg, his uncle Roy is the biggest land-holder. This is like a community with no formal structures, no government or anything, unincorporated. But Roy's like the mayor except 'mayor' doesn't convey it. Chief is closer, as in tribal chief."

He shook his head and closed his eyes and pinched his nose between his thumb and forefinger. "Anyway, Rich had it in for me ever since I came. No particular thing but you know, my education, city background. Roy and the other men, they rib me about being a tenderfoot sometimes but they always help out. Like—it doesn't matter, does it? But Rich was a jerk, I was just somebody he could feel superior to because I was different, you know?

"That night in the Running Iron, I knew right away he was going to start a fight. He was spoiling for it. I suppose I could have just left but that felt like chickening out and he had me pretty pissed off. I don't know, he kicked the living shit out of me, I had a couple of broken ribs, you know, and my nose." He touched it again. "Everybody knew."

Paulie was no fighter. "How big was he?" I asked.

"A couple of inches taller than me. I guess he outweighed me by maybe fifty pounds, something like that. He made me hurt, his fists were so damn heavy."

"So when he was killed near your house with your ax a few minutes after you two had another argument, they picked you up and charged you with his murder."

Paulie barely moved his head. He was staring at the table. It sounded bad to him, too.

"They read you your rights?"

"Yeah, I think so. Yes."

"What questions did they ask?"

"If I wanted to say what had happened."

"And?"

"Yeah, I told them I hadn't done it. What else could I say?"

"Nothing, good. Did they seize the clothing you had on?"

"They made me change, yeah."

"Were your clothes bloody, Paulie?"

"I had helped carry Rich the last few feet into my house, there was some of his blood on my shirt and pants, yeah. They ran some tests on my hands too."

"Paul, do you know who killed Rich Hanna?"

He shook his head. Then he finally sat down. "I don't know, Bunko, I mean a lot of people didn't like Rich. But kill him? I don't know."

"They treating you okay?"

"Treating me . . . ?" He looked at me uncomprehendingly. "What the fuck, Ben? I'm in jail for a murder everybody's sure I did," he said, his voice rising frantically. "I'm terrified of some of the bad asses I've seen in here, a few of them are getting ready to make a move on me." He sobbed, then shook his head fast as if to banish the momentary weakness. "When I defend myself . . ."

I took hold of his wrist across the small table. The red denim was coarse. "I'm sorry, Paul, it was a stupid question." We sat silently for a few moments, our hands clasped tightly.

"Listen," I said, choking back tears of emotion, but laughing, "do you want me to call Estelle?"

Paulie buried his face in both his hands and said nothing. When he finally looked up his eyes were red and swollen but he had regained some self-control. "Poor Estelle is going to age ten years if she hears I'm in jail for murder."

"On the other hand, she'll debone us neat as a pullet if we don't let her know. I'll tell you what, why don't we wait until you're back home and call her then? At least you won't be locked up."

"Yeah, okay," Paul said. "I'm not thinking very straight. I mean I may not even have a house anymore."

An old speaker, painted the same faded and streaked yellow as the walls, screeched high up in the corner of the room behind some more heavy mesh, making us both start and look up. A metallic voice said, "Fifteen minutes to shutdown. Prisoner must terminate interview."

This time we joined all four hands, like we were playing a game of two-on-the-world.

"Listen," I said after a moment, coughing to clear the lump out of my throat. "You want me to go up to your place and take anything away with me?"

He thought about it.

We heard the key in the lock. The door swung open. The sergeant's star was back on his uniform breast, gleaming bright as his skull under the surgical light of the interview room.

"It's okay," he said, standing. "I'll see you in the morning?"

"With Braunstein. Here, don't forget the cigarettes."

The sergeant led Paulie away. I stayed put, hating the suspiciousness that was an occupational hazard. In my heart I knew I wasn't satisfied by the story Paul had told me.

Four

Braunstein got the judge to agree to a ten thousand dollars bond, greatly relieving me. I hadn't told Paul that bail is sometimes refused in murder cases; but Jake trotted out Paul's property ownership in the community and his well-known history of washing behind his ears at bedtime. More important, the prosecutor's protest was perfunctory.

While Braunstein was going through the mechanics of arranging for Paul's release, I crossed a bleak, functional mall where a bunch of chattery birds were sitting on a telephone wire making a din, a case of nature mocking man and his machines I thought anthropomorphically, and paid a visit to the sheriff of Monterey County, R. Roger Etter.

Etter turned out to be a studiously unreadable man in a studiously unreadable office that lacked even the obligatory wife-and-kids framed Kodachrome. The all-government issue blond wood and Naugahyde office made you wonder if he had any family, or merely lacked all vestiges of sentimentality, and the little puzzle gave him an opening advantage over his visitors who found themselves pondering over the man before anything else. Mysteries are a form of power.

"This is about that boy Richards who murdered one of the Hannas over Scottsburg, isn't that right"—He glanced at my card—"Henry?" Then he looked at his watch.

I got all the messages he was sending. First, he knew all about it, so save my breath. Second, I didn't warrant a *mister*. Third, he was a busy man.

I bit my tongue and reminded myself this was about Paulie. I could use R. Roger's cooperation, and asking him what was so piss-poor about his first name he couldn't use it probably wasn't the most direct route to his cordiality. Mentally I took my hat in hand.

"I think you've got the wrong man in custody, Sheriff." Right to the point but sincere and polite.

"Do you now?" He did not agree with me.

"I know how this must sound and usually I wouldn't bother you by telling you the defense thinks the defendant is innocent. But this is a special situation, I've known Paul Richards a long time. You haven't, and you have good reason to suspect him. But I just want to let you know it wouldn't hurt if you looked into it a little further.

"Paul did go out there and confront Rich Hanna but when Hanna persisted in bulldozing a particular tree, Paul slammed his ax into it in frustration and went back inside."

"Uh huh," he said. He was indulging me. Hell, I wasn't entirely sold myself. "Have you checked that tree to see if there's a fresh gash?" I asked.

"You got any idea how many boys put axes into trees? Anything else?"

"I'm just trying to be cooperative, Sheriff. Because you're headed toward being a guy with his dick in his hand who swears he's getting laid."

He smiled tightly. "Okay, I get your message, you got strong feelings about this. I hear that. Now what I got is only three little things. I got a motive. I got an opportunity. And I got a weapon. What you got that beats that?" He stood up but remained behind his desk. Our eyes met coldly. "My door is always open," he said.

I got to my feet too.

"One other thing you don't understand because you aren't from around these parts, Henry," he said neutrally, slipping his hands into his pockets. "This fire, all leave is canceled, there's no vacations and this is August, my men are getting by on no sleep and no overtime 'cause the county can't afford it. That wind shifts, or the line don't hold in the north, we're going to have ourselves a situation down in Carmel Valley. Your friend picked a bad week. If he wants special attention for parking his ax in a red zone he should of done it when all hell wasn't breaking loose in my county."

Five

We drove Jake back to the airport outside Monterey. On the way he questioned Paul and I could tell he was hoping to find a defense based on the right of a man to defend himself against the threat of deadly force. If Rich had given Paul good cause for suspecting he or his house were about to be bulldozed as well as the oak tree, that would be a big help in court.

After Braunstein left we rode on in near silence. Paul was worried about his home, sunk in his troubles, and impatient to be back where the fire was. I started to smell smoke in the air just after we passed through Carmel Valley.

At the turnoff to Scottsburg from the G16 the state police had set up a roadblock. Paul explained where we were headed.

"I wouldn't recommend taking this car up that way," the trooper said politely.

"Oh, this isn't a car, officer," I said. "This is a mobile metaphor."

"Whatever kind. Well, it's your own business." He waved us on.

We drove by a large pasture that was apparently being used as the command center and base camp for the fire-fighting effort. It was noisy as a busy construction site. Noisier. Khaki barracks tents on raised platforms ran away from the helipad in straight ranks, and I spotted a field kitchen, latrines, a convoy of troop transports taking on men, a staging area for vivid yellow fire trucks and red tankers, a small mountain of orange canteens, and jeeps as thick as ants at a picnic hurtling from place to place. A line of men in bright red helmets were jogging toward a waiting helicopter. It was my first glimpse of the magnitude of what was going on, and it took me aback.

The road was very poor and we had to give way to some other truck, tanker, transport, or jeep at almost every curve, so I was creeping anyway when Paulie said, "Slow down here, you'll tear your tires apart on the cattle guards. They're just around the next bend in the road."

We crossed first one cattle guard and then another, as the road meandered along a creek bed through a narrow canyon with heavily wooded hills on both sides. Paulie gestured with his chin toward my side. "The Hannas," he said.

I caught a glimpse of people sitting and standing near a house trailer, and an impression of outdoor living quarters: a baby crib, refrigerator, and bedroom dresser; clothes hung out to dry; a tractor and a pickup on blocks being cannibalized for parts; and then, a bit further along, a paddock and barn. Everything about the scene struck me as weathered and well-used and part of a struggle.

"That," Paul said, "is going to be hard."

"You're going to talk to them?" I was a little surprised that Paul would be planning on approaching the family of the man he was accused of killing.

"I suppose. Pull up over here," he said, pointing at a dead-end spur leading uphill toward a couple of homes back in the trees. Paul hopped out. "Be back in a minute," he said, "there's someone I've got to see."

He started up toward a house and I got out to stretch my legs and have a look around. A knee-high sign by the road said this was Scottsburg; it didn't say how many people lived there. Village was way too big a word for Scottsburg but hamlet might fit. Scottsburg looked to be a triangle of dirt with some waist-deep weeds and clover. From the empty, weathered cable spool at the narrow end, on which somebody had placed a potted begonia, to the row of star-route mailboxes at the base was a distance of perhaps one hundred feet. The only business was a small snack stand. It was closed and shuttered.

The air was hot and close and country quiet. I leaned against the hood of my car and a moment later a lizard the size of a pinky flashed out of the clover and tall weeds, briefly looked me over, and disappeared again.

The smoke was dense this deep into the forest and I could smell burning. The daylight was obscured by a smudgy, oily sky. It was midday and I knew the sun was still shining and the sky blue five miles away; but here the sun was no more than a dully glowing reddish sphere. Again, my understanding of the scope of the fire was enlarged.

Voices reached me from around the next bend, a kind of chanting, and a line of ten or twelve fire fighters in yellow jackets and black helmets jogged into sight in ragged formation chanting, "Hup, hup, hup." At the weedy triangle they broke rank and began to flop on the ground, some not even bothering to remove their packs. Their tools—shovels and axes and some kind of curved hoes—made a clatter. They were plainly exhausted.

The one closest to me propped his head on his elbow, unscrewed the top from a canteen, and took a long swallow.

"You been fighting the fire?" I asked.

"Tennessee hotshots," he said proudly. He was just a kid and his face and clothes were soot smudged. His hair was matted and looked like he'd been through a dust bath.

"Man," said the hotshot beside him from flat on his back, "I'm gawna sleep for two blamed days. How long since we been asleep?"

"Since they brought us," said the first. "Prob'ly was Wednesday, Purv, Wednesday afternoon, right?"

"Cain't hear," Purv said. "Cain't see, cain't talk, cain't think. Was Tuesday."

"We was up on that ridge," the first hotshot said to me, nodding vaguely toward the road. "Clearing brush. You know what they call that ridge, Purv?"

"The one we was on? I don't know. Hell, I don't care none either."

"Well, I was on the same blamed ridge, wasn't I?"

"Yeah," said Purv, "but I didn't know you was there until they brought in that infrared chopper. That baby was developed in Vietnam, you know that?"

"You cain't hardly see your own hand up on the line, I can say that for sure," he told me. "Me 'n him, half the time all I seen was his teeth."

Paulie was coming back down the footpath into the woods talking with a woman dressed in denims and cowboy boots. She was almost as tall as he was. I said so long to the hotshots and walked over to meet them near the car.

When they reached me Paul said, "Lil, this is Ben. My friend Ben Henry."

"Hello." She extended a hand. She had lots of dark blond curls in a kind of halo and a fresh, fair complexion. There were smile lines at the corners of her eyes that made her look pleasantly experienced, and I would have guessed her age to be maybe twenty-seven or twenty-eight.

"All right," Paul said to her, continuing their conversation. "We'd better get up there if you think he may still be there."

"He's driving a boss but that's not until later," Lil said. "He's gone up there every chance he's had since they took you away and Sue and I drove up last night around seven to check on your sprinkler system and whatever. She hesitated. "It's really hard to believe it's you they're saying did this thing, Paul. You had a chance to think much about Roy and Eve?"

"How are they reacting? Do they think I killed Rich?"

"I don't know for sure, it's complicated for them I think, really complicated. Annie's probably the angriest, I'd say to keep an eye out for Annie."

"Annie?" Paul sounded surprised. "Okay, thanks. My phone still working, d'you know?"

Lil laughed. "Glenn and Sue's is. Sometimes anyway."

"I'll see you later," Paul said. "Let's go, Bunko."

"Glad to meet you," Lil said to me.

"Likewise."

I put the car in gear and edged slowly back onto the road. Past Scottsburg it was no longer maintained. I proceeded cautiously. "Are you and she an item?"

"Me and Lil? No, unh-unh. She drives the school bus. I was actually looking for Glenn; he said he'd keep an eye on my place. Glenn Hittel. Glenn's my best friend up here, I suppose. Lil said the fire hasn't reached me yet and Glenn's up there now. Did you follow all that about Roy and Eve and them?"

"Only a little."

"Roy Hanna you know about, our local chief, Rich's uncle. Eve's his wife. She's got cancer by the way, they were just down at one of those laetrile clinics in Tiajuana getting treatment for her. Annie Bayard, the one Lil said was the angriest with me, she's Roy's forewoman. She came up here as a nurse for Eve and still helps look after her, but she grew up on a ranch over in the Salinas Valley and Roy calls her his forewoman.

"She was dating Rich but there's been bad blood between them for awhile. It's not general knowledge I don't think but Sue, Glenn's wife, told me they broke up after Annie had an abortion.

"Drive real slow on this unpaved road, Bunko, a lot of stones and gravel kick up and metaphors are so easily damaged if they get too roughly mixed."

It was the first time he had tried to be funny. Poor Paulie, what a lot of trouble was piled at his doorstep.

"Dammit, Paulie, I'm sorry."

"The only way I can proceed and not lose my mind is to do one thing at a time, Bunko. That's what I'm trying to do. First the house, then I'll see. You're here, that's making a difference. That's the road to my house right there, I'll unlatch the gate."

He jumped out and swung open a locked gate and we followed a steep, rutted path down into a pretty little canyon with a log bungalow in the middle of a clearing. A stream ran through within about fifty yards of the house; the near bank was lawn and the far side wooded. Everything we could see— the sloping roof, Paul's red Bronco and a VW bus, even the leaves on the trees—were coated with a fine gray ash.

The door was on the far side of the house and we had just pulled up when a man came walking over to us from that direction. I knew he must be Glenn Hittel. He was long-boned and knobbly in a solid sort of way, and wore a straw hat with curled brims and deep creases in the crown. The hat was sweat-stained and had a show-offy red feather in the band.

"Shoot, buddy, they kept you down there long enough," Glenn said. He had a nice lopsided smile and deep-set, bulging eyes with large whites. There were a lot of lines worn in his suntanned face, more than a city man of the same thirty-seven or so years would have. Paul had called him his "best friend," a curiously childish coinage that had provoked a childish jealousy in me. I found myself resentful of Glenn for no good reason.

"I'm glad you're back is all. I'm due up at Valley Oak camp. That John I'm driving for, that division boss? About the dumbest sucker I've ever met, just moody and no-command." He took off his hat to scratch his scalp and I was surprised he was bald on top; thick brown curls grew around his ears.

"I think they put him on because they knew he'd screw up," Glenn said. "Like last night we were up in Spiller Canyon, right in there above Carmel Fork where I caught that eight-pound steelhead last year, the one that took a Gray Ghost, you remember, and the wind was blowing hot embers across the line—some of them a foot to eighteen inches long and six inches around. This sucker John, he sat there and watched the fires they set, the slopover, burn. I said to him,

26

'Why don't you put those fires out?' You know what he said? He said, 'Why should I? It's going to burn anyway.'

"Like somewhere up high," Glenn continued, "they must of said, 'We're going to let it burn. We're goin' to get rid of all that fuel and let it burn.' That's what they're doing but they can't go into Monterey or CV and tell people. But that's what they're up to, for some darn reason."

Glenn spoke with a lot of urgency.

"Where is it now?" Paul asked.

Glenn dropped to a knee. His Levis were worn almost white and there was a red corduroy patch on one thigh. He had a rose-colored bandana tied with a knot around his neck. In the dust he began to draw a crude map with a long index finger.

"That's us. Here's the creek, okay? Black Oaks camp. Spiller Canyon. The Apple Thicket. Right here's where it was this morning when I was coming down, about seven-fifteen or so. What happened is about three in the morning the wind came up and the darn humidity dropped to below seventy. Whew! If you're looking for perfect fire conditions, that's it. I saw flames three hundred fifty to four hundred feet high along that entire line from Spiller Canyon over to the Apple Thicket. Man! It is hot.

"There's hotshots in here from all parts of the United States, some boys from as far away as Minnesota, and they said it was the goddamnest fire anyone of them have ever seen.

"It may come in here across the ridge tonight, Paul. Tonight's going to be weird. Really, really weird."

Six

"You hungry?" I asked Paul when Glenn had driven off in his van.

Paul's cabin was built into a hillside. You entered upstairs into a room with a high, sloped ceiling. The space was divided by a breakfast bar into a kitchen area and a dining-sitting room. Outside the wall-length windows was a startlingly close-up view of a garden, lawn, and wooded hillside. We were in a tiny, narrow canyon. A willow dropped sensuously beside the creek that ran through.

"I hadn't thought about it," Paul said. "There's probably some stuff if you want to eat."

The appliances were new but simple, and the cabinetry was oiled pine. Nothing fancy. I went directly to the cabinet above and to the left of the sink where I knew I would find the soup and tuna. The cabinets were arranged like my own, which was to say like Estelle's. I was at home in Paul's house from the moment I walked in. It was a comfortable feeling.

"Paulie," I asked, when I opened the cabinet, "you sure you have enough mayo here? What happens if these three jars run out before you can get to the store?" Paulie had two rules about food: if it's cold put mayo on it, and if it's hot, ketchup. Paul and I were a pair of women-shaped men, as what mother's son isn't?

"I'm going to heat up some tomato soup and make a tuna salad sandwich," I said. He was standing by the long plate-glass windows looking toward his willow. The tree looked pale, as if it were too dry and leeched of some of its color. Just then the sprinklers on the roof kicked in. The spray created the momentary illusion that it had begun to rain just outside the windows and nowhere else.

I mixed two cans of chunk white tuna in a bowl with a squeezed lemon, pepper, and gobs of Best Foods mayo. A celery was standing in a jar of water on the counter.

"Celery?" I asked, mashing the tuna in a bowl.

"Hnuh," Paulie grunted, as if the matter were a weighty one. "Why not?"

"You only live once." I began to dice a celery stalk.

"Bunko, back there in the jail last night you had your suspicions about if I really killed Rich Hanna. Didn't you?" He was still by the windows but looking at me, his arms wrapped around his chest.

I kept dicing celery. "Suspicion is a part of my work, Paulie. The bullshit I hear, it's as reflexive as looking in the rearview mirror when you're driving." I steered the conversation hesitantly toward something I had wanted to say all morning. "One of the things I hate about being a grown man is coming to appreciate rules and procedures you used to scorn.

"Paul, what I'm trying to say is that officially I'm employed by Braunstein, by your lawyer. That means that anything you tell me is privileged, I can't be compelled to divulge it, it can't ever be used against you in any way. I want you to understand that. That's the rule, the rule of law. It's a good rule, but it's only a rule. Whatever happened, I'm with you.

"Now," I said, embarrassed, "you want your bread toasted?"

"No," Paul said. He came into the kitchen and while I ladled the soup into mugs, he sliced some Velveeta onto his sandwich. I never had a Velveeta problem myself.

We carried our lunches across to a round pine table beside the windows in the corner. It was just about dark, outdoors and in, at midday, and we had turned on the lights. A big white globe hung over the table.

Paulie blew on his soup. He sniffed the steam rising off the mug. He took a small sip.

"So?" I asked. "How am I going to find whoever killed Rich Hanna?"

Finally, he met my eye. We both smiled. Our eyes held, and we had conveyed something with elements of love, loyalty, and faith included in it. Under the circumstances it was a nervous exchange. Paulie said, "I think whoever it was, he decided to take advantage of the chaos, you know? The fire and commotion. He was able to kill Rich even though there was a crew working right on the ridge over there, and me around the house here, without any of us noticing. You can see how dark and smokey it is; I can't see all the way to the top of the ridge the way I could if there was no fire."

"You think it was premeditated?"

"It must have been. I mean, a second fight with somebody else within minutes of us almost going at it again? That seems like too much of a coincidence. No, somebody was looking for him and found him just after I left.

"If you had known him, Rich I mean, you'd know it wasn't so farfetched that the woods were crawling with people who'd love to see him dead. Oh man, Bunko," he suddenly cried, "that jail made my skin crawl." He shivered spasmodically and blew a long breath between his lips.

"I hated like hell to see you in there, pally. Though I do think red is really your best color."

Being home had taken some of the desperate edge off his mood, though the danger from Sheriff Etter was as great as ever, and the fire was a palpable presence.

"You know," Paul said, "Rich's own uncle, Roy Hanna, could barely abide the sight of him. If we start asking around we're going to hear about a lot of grudges people had against the guy. Right off the bat there's Annie Bayard, I told you what I heard about the abortion. And driving back I remembered that Glenn told me about a neighbor of his who was ready to kill him over a property line dispute they were having; Peyton's his name. Glenn can tell us more about it. How do you actually go about doing something like this, an investigation?"

"You just ask everybody you can think of a lot of questions. For instance, there were those two hotshots Braunstein said had given statements to Etter. The prosecution'll have to turn the statements over to us and then I'll interview them myself to find out what they really saw. If you've got the right questions they lead you to other people and other questions. It's a lot like reporting except you're able to form conclusions based on instinct."

"What about the sheriff, the authorities?" Paul asked. "Won't they object to us butting into their investigation?"

"I had a talk with the sheriff. He said he was too busy with the fire to bother with your case just yet."

"Good." Paul nodded. "Look, Bunko, here's what I'm thinking, let's start in clearing brush on the far side of the creek, get as much of it as we can out of there. Glenn left us a Pulaski and a mcleod. I should make some calls, too, see if the fire bosses are planning to send a crew up here tonight. And the weather report. Some fog like you have up in San Fran would sure be nice. The sprinkler system is on a five-minute timer and it seems to be working okay but I want to take a close look at it. If the fire comes right down in the canyon here it won't make any difference, but if it stays up on the ridge, keeping the roof wet could save the house."

"A Pulaski, Paulie? Of the Chicago Pulaskis? You're a book editor, what the hell are you doing out here in the woods anyway?"

Paulie rubbed his reddish lips with his knuckles. He fooled around with the pack and lit a cigarette. "I haven't wanted to talk about it especially."

"Well, I knew there was something."

"I'm writing a book," he said. "Downstairs. In the bedroom."

"Ah." It was what he had always most wanted to do.

He leaned his elbows on the table. "Remember when I stayed with you in San Fran two years ago? And I came down here and went hiking in Ventana? Something happened, that's what started the whole thing of giving up my job, and selling off the baseball cards, and coming out here. When I listen to myself like this it sounds so trite, like a midlife crisis or some other ghastly cliché: book editor flees to countryside to write great American blah-blah. But it doesn't feel like that when I'm doing it.

"Okay. What happened, I was hiking. It was a hot day, that was the first summer of the drought, but the creeks were still running and full. I was bent over on my knees drinking from a creek up near Indian Camp and when I looked up there was this mountain lion right across from me, drinking on the other bank. I mean he wasn't much farther away than the fridge over there. My first thought was how well-formed a head a mountain lion had, and how much sleeker and more vital he was than any big cat I'd ever seen in a zoo. I'd never seen a predator that size except in captivity.

"I don't know how come we had both been unaware of each other until that minute, we just had been. I thought my rib cage was going to explode my heart was pounding so hard. Running was . . . I couldn't run even if I had wanted to, my legs were like jelly. And you know, I didn't want to run, not really. I was scared but I wanted to see what would happen. I actually thought, 'Is this how it ends?'

"The lion never looked directly at me. He watched me but kind of at a slant. Such huge, unblinking feline eyes. His alertness was electrifying. Very, very slowly, stealthily really, he picked up his big left forepaw like this, and planted it where he could pivot on it. Then, poof. He turned and ran so fast it was like a disappearing act. Gone! And that's when I smelled him, after he was gone, this strong animal smell that I hadn't noticed until then. He had smelled me, though, and fled from the scent."

Paulie sat upright, realigning himself in the chair. "It was the first time in my life I understood, really understood, what scary goddamn creatures we humans are. Not just the Noriegas and Khadafis and the muggers, but all of us, our whole kind. It made me really sad, you know, Ben? And I thought I should be using my life somehow, instead of just living it.

"The other part was, it made the possibility of my own death more real. I began to tremble. And I knew I was going to come back out here and write this goddamn book that was my secret life."

"Okay!" He sprang to his feet and clapped his hands loudly.

"I hope you brought some knock-around clothes with you, Bunko. I'm going to show you about Pulaskis and mcleods and things. It's callous-growing time in Scottsburg."

Seven

A mcleod—it was pronounced mac-cloud—turned out to be a two-headed torment device. You used one blade like a hoe to cut grass and underbrush, then flipped it to rake away what you had cut with its long, heavy tines. I hated outdoorsy work and always had, but most people, seeing that I was well over six feet and in reasonable shape, assumed that I could toss around bricks, fishing lines, and hoes with the same dexterity I brought to four-wheeled metaphors and basketballs. After a couple of hours of clearing potential kindling from Paul's property while swatting mosquitoes the size of softballs and trying to distinguish poison oak from the other inedible vegetation, I was drenched with sweat, sore and aching in the arms and shoulders, and vile tempered.

We worked hard and without stopping, Paul swinging his Pulaski like a man possessed, cutting roots and grubbing them out of the ground with the curved, hoe-like blade. The fire seemed no closer to Paul's little valley, not as far as I could tell anyway, but its presence was a constant; we breathed smudge-pot air and our eyes smarted and became bloodshot. By the time the dim red sun was gone from view—though whether it had set behind the western ridge or finally been swallowed up in the dense, opaque sky I wasn't sure—we had cleared a two-foot wide zone along the streambed extending perhaps fifty yards upstream from the house.

At last Paul swung his blade into the top of a stump with a strength and finality that made me wince and hope Sheriff Etter never saw him do it just that way. It gave me renewed pause, too—and that made me feel disloyal. He went inside, returning in a moment with two cans of beer. I popped mine and drank off half of it in a swallow.

"You feel it in your arms," Paul said, grinning his warm, crooked grin. "How're your hands?"

"I'm afraid to look." I pulled off the thick cotton gloves Paul had insisted I wear and found lumpish white blisters the size of quarters on both my palms, and raw areas where the skin had been scraped away including one painful one in the V between my thumb and forefinger.

I noticed for the first time that Paul's palms were leathery with callouses; nor was he as tired as I was. In fact he continued to grin at the sorry state of my hands as if the hard work had banished his troubles. He rolled the beer can between his palms.

"I'm going to call Estelle," he said. "Then I thought we'd head down to the Hanna place. There's a hotshot crew coming up here in a few hours, we have to be back when they get here. You want to clean up?"

The bathroom was downstairs beside Paul's bedroom. Paul was upstairs calling his mother in Chicago so when I was finished washing I peeked into his bedroom. There was a word processor on a small table backed up against the footboard of the bed, and a swivel-backed, armless secretary's chair. One wall was lined with books on crude board-and-cinder-block shelves.

When Paul saw me coming upstairs he rolled his eyes and shook his head vehemently. "Here's Ben, ask him if you don't believe me," he said, shoving the phone toward me. "Jesus," he said sotto voce, "see if you can't dissuade her."

35

"Estelle?" I asked. Paul held up a beer questioningly and I nodded.

"*What* is going on out there?" Estelle shouted down the line from the house on the north side.

"Well, Estelle, I'm sure Paulie told you. He's got a real good lawyer and we're going to find out what happened."

"If you persist in talking to me like I'm a half-wit, Benjamin Disraeli Henry, I'm going to start crying. Do you hear me? My son is accused of murder, he says the entire forest is burning down around your ears, and the two of you patronize me?"

I could almost hear her drumming her long crimson nails on the Chinese lacquer telephone table.

"Estelle, there aren't any straight answers. This all just happened. I don't know very much about it myself, I've been here less than a day. Paul seems okay under the circumstances, we've been working all afternoon clearing brush, and they're supposed to be sending in a crew of fire fighters to protect the house. We're going to see some of Paul's neighbors soon."

"I've decided, I'm coming out there. That's all there is to it. Get off the line now please so I can make my reservation. Good-bye."

"Estelle," I cried. "Wait. That's impossible." I fished for some explanation but couldn't think of any. "There's no motel within fifteen miles and Paul has only the one bed." Lame, and Estelle knew it.

"I'll sleep in Paul's bed and you boys can camp in sleeping bags on the floor the way you always used to. And don't you try to handle me like I'm one of your chickies. Did you hear what my son said to me? He said, 'Now is not the best time.' *Now is not the best time.* I could hardly believe my ears. Do you have anything worthwhile to tell me before I hang up? Do you?"

"Estelle, listen, I—"

"I didn't think so." There was a click as she replaced the receiver and then a dial tone. I hung up.

"Well?" Paul said.

"She's booking a flight. Nothing's changed since we were thirteen, we can sleep on the floor."

Paul shrugged, a resigned gesture. "She'll cool down and stay put. She's afraid of crawly, creepy things and I told her the fire is driving the spiders and centipedes into the house, and rattlesnakes are slithering around on the lawn."

Paul and Estelle had a prickly and difficult time of it. They were unspeakably close and Paul often felt suffocated. He was always trying to put enough emotional or geographic distance between them to enable him to breathe freely; the trouble was whenever he succeeded he began to feel guilt and worry about his mother on her own, though in fact she had a thriving art gallery and seemed entirely capable to everyone in the world except her son.

I slipped into a black turtleneck and a leather windbreaker and we drove down the unpaved road toward Scottsburg in Paul's Bronco. Paul was silent. I kneaded my triceps and shoulders, easing the soreness. Near a crude, hand-carved sign that said Hanna Ranch he pulled onto the shoulder and stopped. I followed him up a dirt driveway where our every step raised a small cloud of dust.

We emerged into an enclosure shaded by a towering old oak. At the back of the shallow enclosure an almost vertical hillside created a natural elliptically shaped encampment. Smack dab in the middle was an old, fifties-style house trailer painted green; a refrigerator and a freezer cabinet stood beside it, hooked into its electrical current.

Quite a few people were standing or sitting around on logs and stumps and lawn chairs, and all of them were watching our approach. I admired Paul's courage. Nobody spoke as we drew closer. The people were loosely arranged around a sawed-off metal trash bin, inside of which a blackened stump was smoldering. A big old black coffeepot was perched on the edge of the bin.

The first to approach us was a Chesapeake Bay retriever who loped over and sniffed at my boot. Then he flopped beside two other Chesapeakes with a grunt, as if the effort had bored and exhausted him.

A man dressed in black from his ten-gallon hat to his pointy-toed boots pushed himself off the rusted fender of a Ford pickup on blocks, and walked deliberately toward a Jeep with a padded roll bar, slammed his door, and drove away. His apparent disapproval added tension to the silence.

"Hello, Roy," Paul said. "I came by to tell you I'm sorry about what happened to Rich. I'd have come sooner but they held me overnight in the jail in Salinas."

Still, nobody responded. The women were clustered around a picnic table and a folding card table piled with food and condiments, oil lamps, baby bottles, paper plates and plastic utensils, and a heap of other domestic items. They kept their eyes off us and on what they were doing. The men were mostly on the other side of the smoldering log, under the branches of the oak. The branches were hung with an old creel whose bottom had rotted out, and bridles and cinches and other horsey equipment. We were all waiting to hear from Roy Hanna, the patriarch of this clan, and the man to whom Paul had addressed himself.

Hanna was tilted back in a lawn chair with his cowboy boots pushed against a cooler chest, holding a coffee mug. The mug said PAW in block red letters. His other hand was hooked into his belt, which had a brass buckle in the shape of a bucking bronco cutting into his hard medicine-ball belly. His straw cowboy hat was sweat-stained and pushed way back. You could see the red line around his forehead where the hat usually rested; above the band his otherwise dark, leathery skin was milky white. He had a deeply lined face, a thrust-forward chest, and watery-blue eyes.

"Ain't you got time to sit down and stay some?" he asked, and it was as if a starter's bell had rung and the human race resumed, all the still-life humans going back to whatever they had been doing before Paul's approach. Hanna reached down to scratch behind the ear of a retriever up on his haunches beside his master's chair, his tongue lolling wetly. "Eve, see if these boys want sumpin'."

Paul took a seat on a short bench, and I occupied an empty lawn chair. "This is my friend Ben Henry, Roy," Paul said. "He's down from San Francisco." As I acknowledged the nods of greeting I noticed for the first time that Glenn was there too, sitting on the far side of the smoldering bin with a gold can of Miller in his long hand. He caught my eye and winked and I smiled. His familiar face was curiously reassuring: his expression revealed a secret amusement, and an exaggerated manner of drawing you into the joke.

"Well, I told him," Roy Hanna said, apparently continuing a conversation underway until we had interrupted, "if this forest burns up it'll be because of the damn fire fighters. I don't mean the men, the men are doin' the best job they know how, I mean the ad-min-is-trators. They got about two hundred chiefs falling all over each other. You know, the forest service been trying to blackmail me for years, they'll say, 'You give us a right of way through here, we'll pay for your cattle guards.' Yeah, and if I turn over the right of way, the next thing they'll say will be, 'Move your stable up the ridge, Roy, we need to widen our road.' "

Everybody laughed but the showiest display of agreement came from the only woman sitting with the men. She was dressed in faded Levis and cowboy boots like the men were, and had a straight jaw and a squarish head that made her appear masculine despite her small pretty features.

"I was talkin' this mornin' to this boss," Hanna continued. "He says, 'What we're doin', Roy, is trying to save the forest and protect the watershed.' They talk awful easy to you. I had to tell him, 'You cain't run them nines over the meadow, I know you're fixin' to try.' I told him straight out, I'd shoot the first man runs his tractor on my land. Hell, this forest'll be okay, Mother Nature will see to that. But I got less'n three inches topsoil up there."

He might have been speaking Portuguese for all I understood. He wasn't talking to any one person but to the group at large, holding forth.

"I seen that boss you mean, Roy," Glenn said. "He's so thin he wouldn't make a shadow in moonlight."

"Tha's right, tha's the one," Roy nodded.

Over by the tables a heavyset young woman with long, light brown hair had opened the top buttons of her smocklike blouse to feed an infant. She looked exhausted. A band of children were whooping and playing out behind the trailer, I could hear their shouts and cries. An older woman was cutting sandwiches, helped by two younger women and a teenage girl. In all there must have been some twenty people gathered in the enclosure. My sense was that at least some of them had been forced out of their homes by the fire, and this was the Scottsburg refuge and gathering place.

"Would you like a sandwich?" asked the older woman, I guessed to be Eve Hanna. She had snowy-white, thinning hair, and was wearing a faded floral-print cotton dress. Her face was gaunt and there were deep hollows in her cheeks. She had the shrunken look of a person made suddenly old by pain and illness, and an unhealthy pallor. Looking at her I felt as if my presence here was an intrusion. These people were barely surviving the threat of extinction, they clearly had very little to begin with, and now I was being offered food from their table.

"No thanks, m'am," I said politely, feeling virtuous because the truth was that the brush-clearing and the tension had left me hungry.

"City feller," Roy Hanna said sharply, "Didn't anyone ever teach you better than to say no when you're offered food or drink?"

I smiled at this instruction and the pride behind it. "I guess they didn't. The truth is," I said to his wife, "I'd love a sandwich. And a beer if you have one." Eve brought me a white bread and bologna sandwich thick as a paperback mystery, and a can of Miller, and handed them over without ceremony. I took a big bite out of the sandwich and bright yellow mustard oozed onto my hand. I licked it off.

Eve turned to Paul. "I'm sorry for your troubles."

"Thanks, Eve," he said. "I came over here because I wanted to tell you face-to-face it wasn't me who killed Rich."

" 'Course not, Paul," said a man of about forty standing behind Roy Hanna. "You wouldn't have come around if it was, would you? Pa, I got to be going. I got things to attend to around home."

Hanna's son was six inches taller than his father, with an open, friendly Western American face that would have been right for a Marlboro ad. There was a roll-up cigarette, half-smoked, drooping in the corner of his mouth. All the other men wore baseball-style caps, or else cowboy hats of straw or black felt, but young Hanna wore a greasy, shapeless leather skullcap. The hats seemed to be related to how each man earned his living. The ranchers and hands wore the cowboy hats; those who were employed in local jobs like construction or lumber were capped; and Hanna's headgear probably indicated he was a mechanic, or maybe in heavy equipment.

"When you be back?" Roy asked.

"I don't know. Got to get my three-footer welded, don't I?"

"Awright," said Roy. "We could have to go up the meadow, you unnerstan'?"

"I'll see you, Paul," young Hanna said.

"See you, Roy. Thanks," Paul answered. So the son was Roy, Jr. It said something about him that people didn't call him Junior, it meant that he had earned respect on his own.

When he had driven away, his mother said, "He ain't slept since Tuesday. The men are gettin' tired but the fire isn't."

"You know, I'm sixty-nine years old," Roy Hanna said soberly. "I was born and raised right here, my people been burning this forest since my grandpa came up here from Monterey and homesteaded eight thousand acres for some stupid reason, and the Indians burned before that.

"Fire's a good thing. I seen this forest burn three times in

41

my life and I watched it come back three times too. But there's too much fuel down now and this time it's burning too hot. They ought to allow us to practice burning, but intelligently. You make a fire break at the top, that way the fire you make won't jump it. You make about a mile fire when the wind and the humidity are right, it burns slow. With a couple of men in attendance you can burn a small area very successfully, but the forest service people never understood that.

"And when they finally caught on that burning was the way to keep the fuel down so you didn't get one like this Lost Sam, then they couldn't. See, the Sierra Club, or the Women's League of Voters, all those people wouldn't let 'em. Educated persons with nothing better'n some cause to interest them," he said contemptuously.

"Now when God started this fire with lightning, the forest people have learned their lesson and they're letting it burn. But you could never prove that to anyone because they're spending millions to make it look like they're tryin' their darndest to put it out.

"I tell you one thing, how hot this fire is, it's going to bring back our native grasses. It takes a fire this hot to crack the seed holes so the seed could get moisture enough to germinate. First rain we get in winter, we'll see some grasses we ain't never seen."

"You mean the smooth broom and the foxtail aren't native to this area?" Paul asked.

"These are foreign grasses," Roy said. He leaned closer to Paul and looked intently into his face. "You see, Paul, these grasses came in the sheep the Spaniards brought, they grow too easy, they crowd the others out. Mother Nature got it fixed that way and nobody knows why. The poorer quality grasses crowds out the better and the good seed is down in a hole too thick for the water to penetrate through. But this Lost Sam, it seems like it cracked the seed."

By the time Roy finished it was quiet and tense because of the way the tough old rancher was looking at Paul. Paul's jaw was clenched and his lips pulled thin and he was returning the older man's stare.

Eve Hanna said mildly, "You're being hard on somebody who can't defend himself, Roy."

Just then the younger woman in cowpoke gear abruptly got out of her chair beside Roy and walked away, heading toward the paddock and stable. Roy stared after her. Then he turned to his sick wife, who looked twenty years older than her husband, but wasn't.

"What I'm talking about is our native grasses, old woman. What in hell are you yammerin' about?"

Eve's abiding expression didn't change.

Roy seemed to be saying that the forces of history and nature produced bad seed along with the good, and were beyond the ability of men to account for or combat. Sometimes the bad seed was stronger; seed lines perished and were destroyed. I thought what he meant was that whatever had happened between his nephew and Paul was predetermined. His nephew had been bad seed and there was nothing anybody could do to change that.

Eight

The conversation around the smoldering ash can turned toward the high cost of ranching cattle and the best method of castrating a pig, matters that seldom arose in my part of San Francisco. I stood and made elaborate stretching motions to semaphore my intention, then strolled off in the direction of the paddock.

As I passed his chair I sensed that Paul, thinking I was bored, was going to come along with me, and since I didn't want him to, I pushed gently but firmly down on his shoulder and walked by. He looked questioningly at me but stayed put. I went after the cowgirl I thought must be Annie Bayard, Roy Hanna's "forewoman" who had aborted the late Rich Hanna's offspring.

I found her in the stable examining the hoof of a horse, though what species of horse I couldn't say. It was a deep-chested chestnut with a wheat-colored mane and long, rippled muscles; as I approached it pricked up its ears and whinnied nervously.

"Lookin' for something?" Annie asked, clearly not pleased to see me.

"I was hoping you'd have a minute to talk." Just like horses people study strangers for signs of threat, so I spoke quietly and smiled in what I hoped was an avuncular fashion.

Annie glanced regretfully down at the hoof she was holding and let it drop. " 'Bout what?" she asked, patting the horse's sleek, strong neck. It danced a nervous jig.

"Pretty horse," I said, no doubt impressing the hell out of her: sharp San Francisco guy knows there's a kind of horse that doesn't come in glassine envelopes.

"Threw a shoe coming down off the Meadows. All our horses made it down on their own, 'cept fer a couple old ladies still up there somewheres. Ain't that right, Samantha?" She spoke to the horse because that was easier than speaking to me.

"Just what is the Meadows?" I asked. "Roy said something about it back there too."

Annie toyed with a bridle in her hands. The nails were cut short and the hands were squarish. They looked to be capable hands.

"Meadows is 'bout the only thing that stands between this family and the poor house," she said. "Forty acres of pasture growing in three inches of topsoil, the only good topsoil from here to the ocean." She took a deep breath and let it out loudly. "You didn't follow me out here to talk about Hanna Meadows. You're a friend of Paul's right? Him being a murderer, that don't make no difference to you?" Red spots flushed in both her cheeks.

"You sound as if you're absolutely convinced Paul murdered Rich."

She swiveled suddenly and whacked the bridle against the gate of the stall, startling Samantha who began to dance again and protest loudly. Annie made shushing sounds. "We don't have criminals around here," she said.

"I grew up with Paul," I said, "and I don't think he has murder in him. I know how it looks but Paul did not kill Rich."

"I tell you what we say, mister."

"Sorry, I should have introduced myself. I'm Ben, Ben Henry."

"If it looks like a pig, and sounds like a pig, and smells like a pig, then it's a pig."

"We say something like that in San Francisco, too, but we say that it's probably a pig. It could just be some other animal that wants you to think it's a pig. Listen, Annie, the reason I wanted to talk is that I'm working for Paul's lawyer, trying to find out what actually happened. I'd appreciate it if you could help me. What kind of man was Rich Hanna?"

Home movies ran through her dark eyes. She took off her hat and tugged at the hair behind an ear. The hair was coal black, like her eyes, and cut in short bangs. It was fine, flouncy hair, and the hat was standard-issue black felt, the same as a lot of the men wore. She had on Levis and there was a bright red bandana held in place by a knot at her throat. Annie was built narrow and sinewy through the shoulders and waist, but her hips and thighs flared unexpectedly and gave her a bottom-heavy appearance. I would have said she was in her mid-thirties. Despite the angry set to her mouth I was hoping the need to talk would outweigh her mistrust for me.

"It ain't fair to call Rich some kind of bad seed, the way Roy said back there. Rich's dad was a drunk, he used to beat Rich black and blue when he was on the booze. Last we knew 'bout him he was over Stockton direction, washing dishes or something. Rich's mom ran off with a long-haul driver when he was eleven. Roy and Eve, the Garbers, his kin, they kept their eye on him from then on in. It shamed him. He didn't like the pity." She shook her head. "Rich had a mean streak he must of got from his dad and he could be a bastard. But if you cared 'bout him he'd care back when he wasn't too drunk or stoned or hung over, which was most of the time."

"The way you talk about him, I think you cared a lot about him," I said.

"Matter of fact, I couldn't stand the sight of him."

"Why'd he beat Paul up like that?"

"In the Running Iron that time? It's like I said, Rich was

mean when he got drunk. Your friend Paul, he wasn't from around here and he wasn't the first rich man to come around here either. This here's beautiful country but it's rugged and wild back in these mountains and people like that don't last long. Most folks here live by the skin of their teeth."

"But Roy and Eve seem to have accepted Paul well enough, why's that?"

"Roy took a shine to him, that's true, was part of why Rich kind of felt the way he did. Your friend paid Roy a lot of respect, asked his advice about everything, brown-nosed him. Roy's sort of the oracle, I'm kind of his mouthpiece." She couldn't disguise the pride she took in being the oracle's mouthpiece.

"So Roy liked Paul better than his own nephew, and Rich resented Paul for that?"

"Paul was a rich man from the city, Rich said, what was he doing around here anyways? Scottsburg just was no place for him."

We were leaning with our backs against adjacent stalls. She was still toying with the bridle and I had my hands in the pockets of my jacket; we had to look sideways to see each other, which I found awkward but seemed to make talking easier for her. The stable smelled of straw and oats and animals and dung. It was a deep, satisfying smell. Horses nickered in a few of the stalls.

"You live around here all your life?" I asked her.

"Grew up in the Valley over King City way," she said. "I was nursing up at San Jose in South Hill Medical Center when Roy started bringing Eve round for treatments. Before I knew it I was back down here working for Roy and caring for Eve. I was about fed up, and Roy's a persuasive man."

I glanced over at her, curious about something unexpectedly warm in her tone and saw a secret little smile hover around her eyes and lips. Was she Roy's lover?

"Eve doesn't look very well," I told her.

"Eve's got pancreatic cancer. We been down to the clinic in Tijuana. We were planning on goin' fishin' over in Baja but we had to come on home because Eve was doing poorly. But she's all quieted down now and the laetrile shots are seeming to help. She put on two pounds."

I wondered if Annie had been around when Rich was killed. "When did you get back?"

"Last Wednesday I guess it was, day before this Lost Sam." She pushed herself off the stall posts and reached for a bucket on a peg. The horses began to dance and mutter and make a racket. "I got animals to tend to now," she said.

"I don't want to hold you up," I said. "Maybe some other time we can talk again. Thanks for helping."

She shook her head and was unlatching Samantha's stall as I walked out of the stable and started slowly back toward the family enclosure.

My sense was she had withheld far more than she divulged. It was certainly possible that she had loved Rich Hanna, and if she had that made it more probable that she might have killed him. Places, conditions, times, and events all change, but human nature is always the same: women who kill usually kill men they have loved. Men usually kill other men too: basically if you'd rather not be killed being a man is a bad deal, but when men do kill women they prefer to do it in a bedroom with a gun. Women's room of choice is the kitchen, and their weapon a knife. An ax, I supposed, qualified as a heavy knife and I would have thought a ranch forewoman strong enough to swing it in anger. Anger was just one in a snakepit of emotions I had felt roiling inside Annie Bayard.

The woman was hiding something, I was certain of it.

Back at the enclosure the men were engaged in that time-honored pastime, bitching.

"You cain't make enough off the cattle in this country to pay fer taxes let alone support the family," Roy Hanna was saying as I sat back down. "You know, buy groceries and cars and clothes and all that stuff everybody else has. I know of only two ranches in this whole country that are self-sustaining. Now twenty, thirty years ago this whole country was cattle."

"How do people get by then?" I asked, joining in.

"A lot of people here are on construction," Glenn said. He had an ankle crooked over a knee and was slouched down in his chair. "Sum folks are on welfare, a lot of people around here are really fed up with what's going on and just living and trying to be pretty quiet about it," he said with that smile like a wink that drew you in. "I don't know how many families we got—"

"More dogs 'n people," said a man I hadn't seen before, a skinny guy with a long nose wearing a yellow jacket.

"—but we're like one family," Glenn finished.

"To my way of thinking," Roy said, "this country is only good for recreation or residential. The only crop I ever saw make any money for anybody was mary-juana."

Paul smiled. "Did you ever smoke marijuana, Roy?"

"Weh-ul, I tried it once or twice. Trouble was," Roy drawled, "whenever I smoked it I forgot my hat."

When the appreciative laughter died down, Roy said: "If they legalized it they wouldn't make no money off it either, 'cause the Salinas Valley farmers would grab it wall-to-wall. Quality wouldn't be any good but they'd have so much of it people's markets would collapse, just like any crop. I don't think there's that much mary-juana left anymore in this country 'cause people are afraid law enforcement's gawna take their land. Ain't that right, Glenn, as far as the thinkin' of gentlemen farmers?"

"I suppose so, Roy, if you say so," Glenn said. "I don't go nowhere near that stuff myself. What I was starting to explain before," he said to me, "was that people in Scottsburg have a real sense of pride and belonging."

Eve Hanna had quietly come to sit beside her husband, in the seat at his right hand, the same one Annie Bayard had vacated. She had been listening to what was being said, and I hadn't expected her to speak at all, except perhaps to offer more food or drink, because her manner was so deferential. I think some of the others were surprised too when she started to talk, because the silence became less companionable and more awkwardly attentive. She had a clear, sweet voice.

"People used to help their neighbors. We would always go to help our neighbors and they would help us too when we needed it. You din't have to ask. And these federal boys, they used to be good boys, they were our friends, weren't they Roy?

"Forty, fifty years ago, you remember. Before they said no burning, when the springs ran and still had steelhead and we ranched five hundred head. Then the taxes went up and up and up and we had to start selling and then people were more to themselves.

"The forest was healthy then. I really had to laugh when they started those signs: THIS IS YOUR FOREST, USE IT. I mean they wouldn't let you *do* anything we used to do."

She wasn't looking directly at any of the men from behind the thick glasses that made her eyes swim like oysters on the half-shell. She rested her arms lightly on the aluminum arms of the lawn chair and looked past us, into the forest. The joints in her fingers were red and swollen.

Roy had his elbows jammed into his knees, and he was staring at the earth between his boots. You couldn't see his face at all, just the sweat-stained crown of his hat.

"No more hunting," Eve said. "No more fishing. No camping 'cept fer their sites. No burning like the men always did. It wasn't natural not letting people use the forest, the Hannas and the Garbers and the Nasons and folks from here round. And you know without people the forest just goes right down, right down. The federal people is the ones who let it go, they stopped caring for the trails and springs. Roy always tried to tell them and they would listen and all but those federal boys weren't free to make up their minds, they had the policies." The way she said *policies* it sounded like some bafflingly malign force. Like cancer.

"One time I remember me and Roy had the kids on a picnic

up to Church Creek the rangers wrote on our permit, 'You will not advocate the burning of the forest.' But we knew burning was a good thing, we remembered when you could ride anywhere without trails, and you could run a herd big enough for a family to live on. Mother Nature has lightning to clear out the cluttered places and give them some rest, so when Mother Nature didn't do the job the men took care of it.

"Then they brung in no burning. Now the streams are choked and the deer starve and the trees are so full of disease, it ain't right. This Lost Sam is good for the forest, it's goin' to leave the forest clean and new again. Ain't that right, Roy?"

Eve had grown hoarse from the effort of talking for so long with so much feeling. She was weak and looked shrunken from having slid lower in her chair as she spoke.

Roy stood. He lifted her effortlessly, as if she weighed no more than a small child. "Go bring Annie," he said to one of the young women by the picnic table. Then he turned and carried Eve into the trailer. The screen door swacked closed behind them.

Nine

"Everybody pays court to Roy," I said to Paul when we were back home again.

"He's a mass of contradictions," Paul said. "He's prejudiced against what he calls educated assholes but he insisted his kids finish high school and encouraged Roy Junior to go to college. He's inflexible and judgmental but also kind and generous. He's been generous to me. I guess life's a mass of contradictions and Roy's alive. He's natural, as basic to the forest out here as it is to him."

Paul was pacing nervously and smoking as he talked about Roy. There had been a state fire engine parked up at the gate when we got back, but no crew with it; it was the first time the fire bosses had sent equipment into Scottsburg itself—we had passed trucks and engines stationed outside other residences as well—and it meant that tonight might be the night Lost Sam burned its way to Paul's doorstep.

With the cigarette drooping in the corner of his mouth Paul bounced up on the balls of his feet and began throwing lefts and rights at the air, shadowboxing. We had passed our adolescence like this, shooting the breeze, throwing punches or sinking imaginary jumpshots, living and dying with Ernie Banks and Billy Williams. It was all preferable to homework though in the end Paul always completed his while I called a girl, or read novels in bed. It had been Paul, though, who found the books that meant the most to us then: *Augie March, The Man with the Golden Arm, Catcher in the Rye.*

A deep smokey gloom had settled into the forest, and what light there was was preternatural, the silver darkness that precedes a storm. The night was going to be bad and I was feeling tired at last, the two emotionally grueling days since Paul had called me made my eyes gritty and my mouth dry and metallic. The sprinklers were whirring softly on the roof, and every five seconds a light sheet of water splashed across the garden outside the windows. I couldn't see that this setup would make much difference if a forest fire raged through.

Paul threw three sharp left jabs, stalking forward. He covered up and tucked his head in, peek-a-boo style. He had patterned himself after a light-heavyweight champ named José Torres, who was also a writer. "That fire crew should be here soon," he said. "The fire's moving slow now but when the inversion level drops it'll take off." He dropped his hands to his side. "Just listen to me, Bunko," he said and laughed nervously in his nose. "All of a sudden I've become an expert on the effects of humidity and other weather factors in charting the progress of a forest fire."

"Know thy enemy," I said. "Where is the fire now exactly?" I sensed its presence but without city streets to guide me, and with the sun no longer visible, I wasn't at all sure which way was east and which west.

Paul pulled open a drawer underneath the divider counter that separated kitchen from dining area, and rummaged inside, pushing things out of the way until he pulled out a Geological Survey map. He spread the map in front of us on the pine table.

"You understand topo maps? The squiggly lines are elevations. Where it looks like the inside of a telephone, it's steep."

"It all looks steep then."

"That's why this fire is such a bitch to fight. All they can do is cut lines on the ridges, try to deprive it of fuel, and pray the line will hold. They don't really put it out so much as they contain it until it burns itself out. If it weren't so dry, if the ocean fog would only come in, that would slow it way down.

"Here," he pointed. "This is us here. Facing this way," he said, turning the map on a diagonal axis. "The creek. That hill out there." His finger went across the hill and continued a short distance to the northwest. "That's the forward point of the fire, its southern front. But it's moving on two fronts. The northern front was set by lightning; I'm not sure what got it started in the south, nobody's said. It's moving all along here, from down there in Lost Valley to Uncle Sam Peak."

"Lost Sam," I said, understanding. "Is that how they name them? Not alphabetically like hurricanes?"

He nodded.

"When they started naming hurricanes for men as well as women," I said, "what did you think?"

"That women hold up half the sky," he said, and we laughed together.

"So how far away is it then?"

"A few hours ago it was about a mile." Then he looked up and stared at the obscured hillside, lost in his thoughts. There were no good subjects at the moment unless you considered the promised arrival of his mother, whose idea of roughing it was rain on the day she had her hair done.

"When I went for a walk back there, Paul, I had a little talk with Annie Bayard. She says Rich Hanna resented you because you were rich and an outsider. And because Roy thought more of you than he did of Rich even though Rich was his nephew."

"It's funny, you know. I didn't even know Rich had it in for me until he started that fight. He seemed about as surly with everybody as he was with me."

"Even with Annie?"

"Well, whatever their actual relationship was they weren't

lovey-dovey or anything. Wait," Paul said. "There's the fire crew. I'll be right back." He walked quickly outside and around the house toward the drive. I saw headlight beams bobbing against the murky sky as the fire crew bumped slowly down the approach to the house.

Paul was back in a moment not with a crew of hotshots after all, but with Glenn and Lil, the woman with the blond curls I had thought might be Paul's girlfriend when we had first arrived in Scottsburg from Salinas. She was holding a cake which she put down in the middle of the round table where I was still sitting.

"Hello," she said cheerfully.

"Poppyseed?" I asked, smiling back.

"I don't think it came out right, it's too moist."

"There's no such thing as too moist when you're talking poppyseed."

"It's lemon-walnut," she said.

"Or lemon-walnut."

"That so?" Her smile was amused, and her eyes were heavy lidded in a way that made her seem not tired exactly but drowsy. When she smiled, lines appeared at the corners of her eyes.

"Howdy do," Glenn said, coming in with Paul.

"I'll make coffee." Lil went on toward the kitchen.

"I thought you were driving tonight," Paul said to Glenn.

Glenn gave him a wide-eyed can-you-believe-this smile. He bore some resemblance to Donald Sutherland, the actor. "I know, I know. I swear to Obediah, those suckers are so dumb they must think their Rice Krispies are doughnut seeds. Turns out the way their schedule is set up, they want me in the morning, four A.M. And they don't tell me they switched it around till I get all the way out to Valley Oak. Shoot," he said, shaking his head. "How're them sprinklers working, all right?"

"Perfectly," Paul said. "But I want to have a closer look at the pump. Ben was just telling me about a talk he had with Annie."

Lil brought some plates and a slicing knife to the table. "Is it too much trouble for you boys to cut your cake yourselves?"

Glenn took a playful swipe toward her bottom with a big, sun-reddened hand, but she danced easily out of his reach. She moved splay-legged, up on her toes, like a trained dancer.

"Oh, you know what I've been meaning to ask you," I said to Paul. "Who was that who made a show of leaving when you went over to the Hanna's, the guy all in black?"

"That's Peyton," Glenn answered.

"That was Peyton?" I was surprised. "I thought he and Rich had had a property dispute, that they were enemies?"

"Peyton's a funny one," Glenn said. "He's Esalen, y'know?"

Esalen? The mind resort out at Big Sur on the coast? I couldn't imagine the bad-ass cowboy dunking himself all white and naked, or making touchy-feely Jacuzzi talk with stockbrokers from Los Angeles. "Esalen?"

"Yup, pure Esalen on his father's side. His mom Doris is a white woman from over Greenfield way."

Esalen *Indian*. I felt for a moment as if I understood nothing at all, that what I thought I was understanding was all wrong, off-the-mark. What good was I to Paul out here in the woods?

"Peyton's gone back to his roots," Paul said. "He calls himself a medicine man and tries to practice the old tribal ways."

Glenn cut himself a wedge of cake and bit into it. "Made his own business out of it, a dude ranch sort of setup. Gets 'em out in nature and scares the hell out of 'em with chanting and tom-toms and wolf howls."

"I wonder why he made such a show of leaving," I said, thinking out loud. "I mean, does he disapprove of Paul? Really? Or is a good accusatory offense the best defense against suspicion focusing on him? He had a motive for killing Rich, too, didn't he?"

"I suppose he did," Glenn said. "Maybe you got something there. I'll tell you this much, Peyton's one of the only ones in this country who figured out how to make a living just by being who he is. Stopped drinking, too."

"What about Roy, Jr.?" I asked.

"What about him?" Paul said.

"You said he had a college degree?"

"In geology but he's operating heavy equipment now. There they are!" Paul got up and walked out again. You could hear the gearbox of the transport laboring as it downshifted on the steep road in. It was fully dark now and the horizon above the hillside looked like East Chicago where the huge blast furnaces stained the night sky with an ominous orange glow. Glenn unwound his lanky frame, took his cake with him, and followed Paul out.

I wasn't sure whether to go with the men to meet the fire crew or stay put. I started to rise not because I wanted to but because I felt I should, when Lil put a mug of hot coffee in front of me, and a tin of evaporated milk, and sank into the seat across from me. I relaxed where I was, my mind made up.

Lil raised both her knees up under her chin and hugged them, holding her mug in both hands. "What did you think of our Annie?" she asked.

"She seems like she's in turmoil," I said, moving my coffee an inch closer with my fingertips. "I wondered if she was Roy Hanna's mistress."

Lil pursed her lips and blew on her coffee. Her lips were a deep purple-pink, soft and mobile. I hadn't noticed until that moment how sensual they were, maybe because the big owlish glasses made her seem prim at first glance.

"She'd like to be," Lil said. "I think she'd like that a whole lot."

"She told me she was the oracle's mouthpiece, that she spoke for Roy. She was boasting, but then later Eve started talking about the forest and I knew it wasn't true, what Annie had said."

"Tell me about your impressions so far," Lil said. "What did Eve say?" She reached into a pocket of the embroidered gray wool cardigan she was wearing over a white cotton blouse with a scoop neck and pulled out a pouch of Bugle and a blue packet of Zig-Zag rolling papers.

"You mind cigars?" I asked.

"My dad smoked 'em," she said.

I lit up one of my Dunhill Chicos. "We were over there this afternoon and Eve was talking about how the forest used to be before the no-burn policy, how green it was, and clean. Listening to her was like immersing yourself in one of those free-flowing streams she was describing. She was speaking so quietly that everybody had to concentrate on what she was saying; there was something almost mystical about it I thought. The whole time, Roy had his hands clasped between his knees and he was staring at the ground. Annie can call herself anything she wants, but Eve speaks Roy's heart, doesn't she?"

"But you know," Lil said, "Roy's a virile man and Eve's been real sick for a real long time. And she's going to die soon."

I nodded. "She collapsed from the effort and Roy had to carry her inside. He sent someone to bring Annie."

"Annie is real devoted to looking after Eve," Lil said. "She's a nurse, you know. She gives her her shots and she went with them down to Tijuana for the laetrile therapy. She's really attached to that whole family, you see?"

"And Rich? What was that about, Annie and Rich?"

"I don't know exactly. They were both kind of outcasts in the same family. And maybe some of it was a message she was sending to Roy, that she had her own needs too."

I finished the last bite of cake. "This cake's delicious," I said, smiling. "Just moist enough."

She looked pleased and met my smile halfway. "Here, I'll cut you another slice."

"No, I couldn't."

"Oh, go ahead," she cajoled.

We laughed together.

"Just a small one then," I said. I carried both our cups to

the stove and refilled them from the pot. Walking back with a mug in each hand I asked, "She aborted Rich's kid?"

"Yes," Lil said. "Thanks." She relit her roll-up, then leaned back in her chair and tilted it by placing her soles against the edge of the table. The denim stretched over the long swell of her calves. "You seem to have read Annie pretty easily," Lil said.

"Did I?"

We both looked out the open door toward the creek. Down there the flashlights and lanterns of the fire crew bobbed in the darkness. I caught only glimpses of men as a light stabbed an orange canteen or hopped across a bright yellow jacket. I listened to the clump and clatter and mutter of men milling about, organizing themselves to do a job.

"Private eyes don't help on fire lines?"

I turned to face her. She was a woman who changed the more closely you observed her. Until that moment I had been noticing isolated things about her: her halo of dark blond curls, her long dancer's body, her glasses, her taut, tawny skin. Her reserve and something almost prim and proper. Now, suddenly, she coalesced and I was looking at an extraordinarily beautiful woman. Momentarily, out of the habit of my loyalty to Jessica Gage, I looked away. Then our eyes met and I saw Lil's conspiratorial smile, a smile that seemed to see right into my sudden understanding. Something happened. Or I thought it had. It had happened so fast I couldn't be absolutely sure.

"It doesn't come up much in San Francisco," I said. "You're not really from around here, are you?"

She shook her head. "I came down from Berkeley about this time year before last. Sue and I had roomed together years ago—the year she met Glenn, so we all go back a ways together. I needed to get my act together and they had this little place on their property where I had stayed before, the Glass House they call it. They said I could come down and stay, it was only going to be for a couple of weeks maybe." She held her hands out in a here-I-still-am gesture, and laughed in a self-deprecating way.

"You drive the school bus, Paul said."

"I drive the school bus."

"You listen to the kids?"

"Do I ever."

"Who do they think killed Rich?"

"The kids?"

"Kids listen to everything and grown-ups usually act as if the kids won't hear what we don't want them to hear. And then kids get together and they all parrot what their parents said."

She laughed. "You have that right. But school's out, it's August. Kids here, it's not like in Berkeley or someplace big. Death's not a big mystery, the six-year-olds are wringing the necks of chickens and the eight-year-olds are hunting with pellet guns."

She picked up a small gold lighter from beside the pouch of tobacco and toyed with it with long, slim fingers.

"If you're really going to help your friend," Lil said, "you're going to have to think a little differently than the way you would up in San Francisco. People here aren't as bad but they're just as wicked."

I laughed. "That's a neat distinction."

"I'm glad you like it." She held her hand flat over the table. "What you've got to do is remember to zig," turning an expressive palm up, "when maybe you'd have zagged."

Ten

Paul hurried into the house through the open door. "We're going up to the line; here, put these on. There's a boss who said he'll take us up there."

He tossed me khaki pants and a bright yellow jacket, the same as he was wearing. Imitating what he had done, I slipped them on over my jeans and shirt. They fit like a scarecrow costume, my ankles and wrists stuck out comically, and the jacket wouldn't close across my chest.

Lil tried to hide her amusement by looking down at the table and putting her knuckles against her mouth.

"Oh, I'm sorry," she said, gasping, "you just look so ridiculous. There, I'll stop." Instead a peal of laughter bubbled out despite her effort to suppress it. I liked the way she laughed at me, it showed somehow that we had become allies.

"Ready?" Paul asked anxiously.

"Let's go," I told him. I followed him toward the creek bed. Oxygen seemed in short supply in the sooty air. The outfit I had on had been treated with some kind of fireproofing that made the material gritty to the touch. Asbestos probably. My day wouldn't have been complete without exposure to at least one deadly carcinogen.

The sky as we made our way beneath it along the ash-dusted lawn was opalescent behind a curtain of smoke; against its black canvas was splashed an almost liquid play of reds, purples, oranges, and yellows. We stomped through the creek bed where only a trickle of water ran and onto the far bank where Glenn and two men in forest service uniforms were waiting beside a Jeep, its motor idling.

A fire crew was spread out along both banks of the creek, some men talking, some smoking, one on his back with his legs crossed and his head resting against his helmet as he watched the ominous kaleidoscope in the sky.

"Let's hit it," Glenn said.

"This ain't by the book, you unnerstan'," said one of the fire bosses. He was bandy-legged and had a battered nose and scar tissue around his jug ears. He looked as if he had fought as a lightweight. "You boys remember that, look smart if I say."

"Thanks," Paul said. "We will."

The wilderness firemen climbed in front and the three of us wedged ourselves onto a hard bench in back. The Jeep was an open vehicle. The other boss, the one who had not spoken, took the wheel. The back of his neck was minutely seamed and there was a red boil just beneath his hairline. The ex-lightweight was holding a walkie-talkie that crackled and hummed with staccato, static-interrupted talk. The Jeep lurched toward the trees, starting up the ridge, and I realized that there were no roads running to wherever we were headed, only paths.

It was a good thing there wasn't a roof on the Jeep because every jolt sent us flying high above our seats. After my first hard landing had numbed the base of my spine and sent pins and needles through my hands, I concentrated on trying to cushion and minimize the impact. The higher we went, the more the Jeep seemed to be clinging to terra firma through the fly-like gripping power of its wide, deeply rutted tires. Its heavy-duty gearbox labored noisily to pull us up the densely wooded incline, making conversation all but impossible.

Something that looked like a lion shot across the path ahead of us, passing so rapidly through the beams of light cast by the headlamps that I caught only a strobe-like glimpse.

"What the holy hell was that?" I yelled to Glenn beside me.

"Lion," he shouted back. "On the run."

"Oh," I said. I understood, I had seen *Bambi*.

Then we were out of the trees and into what I feared momentarily was the fire itself, so dense was the murk and heavy the heat. I saw that there were men all around, and heavy equipment lumbering, and I realized it wasn't the smoke from the fire alone that made the air fuliginous, it was the thick dust raised by the bulldozers and back hoes as they clanked about their destructive business. To our left five or six machines were working in concert, roaring as they tore up huge old trees like rotten teeth being extracted, and shoved them aside. What was left behind was the fire line, a freeway-wide gash of nothingness.

"Those dumb fucks," Glenn shouted at my ear, pointing. "Can you imagine how many fires those trees survived? I would like to goddamn believe human beings can come into a place and do a job and not destroy it."

The two fire bosses had climbed down, as we had, and were about twenty yards from us. The ex-lightweight was talking into his walkie-talkie, and the taller boss was down on a knee taking some kind of sample in what looked like a plastic belljar. When the lightweight finished talking he waved at us to follow with his walkie-talkie, and started out across the fire line. We clambered after him. It was rough going. Clods of earth the size of mailboxes were upended, gigantic root systems were exposed, and yet I felt as vulnerable as if I had been crossing a freeway in the dark; I kept looking this way and that, worrying that a dozer might bear down on us, the driver unable to see or hear us amid the chaos of heat and noise and sensation.

We reached the edge of the ridge, where the line ended and

the earth fell sharply away. I looked down into the smoke-filled ravine and then out across to another ridge beyond. I thought I was looking west, and that somewhere in that direction, not very far off, lay the Pacific. Being at the mercy of a conflagration and yet so close to a limitless supply of water seemed sublimely ridiculous.

"How far's that next ridge?" I shouted to Paul.

"Black Bear Ridge," he shouted back.

Before I had a chance to explain that I had asked how far it was and not what it was called, a ball of fire so huge it seemed like a full moon rising with a face of flame shot into view above the hilltop and hung briefly in the sky before it burst, shooting orange-red tracers that riddled the downslope of Black Bear Ridge like a machine-gun attack. Trees ignited with a sharp hiss as the oil in the leaves went up in flame. Plumes of whitish smoke curled off the burning trees and were caught in an updraft that pulled them back toward the ridge top. The air felt dry as sand, the fire had sucked the moisture right out of it.

In that instant the entire crest of Black Bear Ridge, which couldn't have been more than a half-mile distant, burst into flame as if the Devil had snapped his fingers. The treetops burned neon orange with yellow licks, and flames made ragged outlines along the long trunks. The fire that was consuming the top of Black Bear Ridge made a deep whooshing roar and hiss punctuated by popping explosions. It was as if an ordinary fireplace fire crackling in the grate had been piped into the firmament through some incomprehensibly huge Dolby system.

"Good God," Paul said reverentially, and it was as though he had spoken my mind. In the face of so awesome a force of nature what I felt most deeply was not danger or fright but humility.

As we stood watching Black Bear Ridge burning, each of us wrapped in his own thoughts but unable to tear our eyes away, the main body of the Lost Sam fire rushed into sight from behind the ridge. It seemed to be swimming across the crest, its long tendrils of flame resembling waves lapping at a shore. This wave of flame dwarfed the fire ahead of it on the slope, the fire that had been so awesome a second before. I saw now that the tracer attack let loose when the gas ball erupted had been an advance party Lost Sam had sent ahead to prepare its own welcome.

"Eighty thousand acres," Paul shouted. "It's burned eighty thousand acres already."

The taller fire boss appeared again, carrying long-handled shovels. "Here," he said, "you men come along, there's a crew shorthanded."

We each grabbed a shovel and followed after him, trotting and stumbling over the churned up earth. As I ran it occurred to me that less than seventy-two hours earlier the worst danger facing me was the silent Italian's razor.

"If it jumps this blame ridge it's got a clear shot to Los Padres," Glenn shouted, jogging beside me.

"Los Padres?"

"The dam," Glenn said, pointing his shovel out into the oily darkness. "Water supply for the whole of Carmel Valley."

As we came up toward the crew we were supposed to join, the forest launched a rocket attack against our position. Flaming embers, some the size of stepladders, some much larger than that, and others no bigger than a softball, whistled through the air and imbedded themselves all around us. Men rushed at the deadly glowing branches and began to pound them into submission using the flat side of their shovels.

"Hot iron, hot iron!" they shouted, as they fell on them.

The smoke was thicker than it had ever been and it stung my eyes and all but blinded me, and I was rubbing futilely when an incandescent hot iron crashed to earth not five feet away. The four of us attacked it, lifting our shovels and pounding it into smaller and smaller embers that glittered and shimmered and then burned into nothingness like faraway stars in another galaxy. Then another hot iron hit, and another, and then I lost count. After that there was only the noise and the effort and the smoke and the knowledge of other men doing what I was doing, chasing after each deadly splinter of fire and pounding it heatless. I'd see one land and run toward it and then begin swinging my shovel side by side with men whose faces I never noticed, all of us shouting, cursing, straining.

Again and again I heard choppers overhead, hovering. Once the smoke blew away almost magically, the air cleared momentarily, and I saw a helicopter dumping billows of bright red retardant into the flames. It seemed like trying to put out a burning building with a blanket.

Beneath me on the ridge slope a crew of hotshots were lashed together on the seventy degree incline, one of them setting the grass afire with a flamethrower burping napalm. The set fires swept downhill toward the inferno in the ravine, and suddenly the actual meaning of back burning became clear to me. It was man-made arson, an attempt to deprive the fire of fuel and turn its course away. The smoke closed over the hotshots on the slope and I raced toward a shower of embers, pummeling them with all my might. But in that brief moment of clearing I had seen how much closer the inferno had advanced, and it gave me a renewed and frantic strength. I banged harder and harder.

There seemed to be more men in my area now, an army of us with faces black with soot and streaked with sweat, all swinging implements. The fire had invaded the floor of the ravine, and through the bank of dense white smoke fiercely orange flames with startling yellow hearts leaped hundreds of feet into the air.

I didn't have a clue how many hours we had been on the line when all at once the pace of activity seemed to slow. The fire still roared and hissed, but the sound was somewhat diminished. The heat eased off and the hot irons were no longer whistling in on long flat trajectories with the same ferocity. Somewhere up-line a man yelled hoarsely, "We won!"

The fire had swum on by, and though the forest in front of us was still burning, the engine of the fire, its voracious appetite, had been held and turned back from the ridge where I stood.

"We won! We won, we beat the sumbitch!"

"Damn! Damn! Damn!" Cries and shouts passed up and down the fire line, and men who had not rested in many hours flopped down without ceremony.

Dragging my shovel I began to walk toward where I had last seen Paul working frantically. I had never been so thirsty in all my life but I had no canteen. Guys were drinking greedily everywhere I looked, men I didn't know and had never seen before, and if our eyes met they gave me huge, black-face grins as I walked by. The feeling of closeness with these strangers was as jubilant as the exhaustion I was starting to feel was pervasive and deep. It invaded every muscle and joint of my body.

I almost fell over Paul. He was sitting slumped over, his legs crossed beneath him. A bright orange canteen lay ignored in his hand.

"Paul?"

He looked up, nodded, but said nothing.

I dropped down beside him, took the canteen from his hand, unscrewed the top and swallowed too much too rapidly. When I finished coughing and choking I tried a smaller sip and then another and another. The warm, ugly-tasting water was fresh and satisfying.

I turned to Paul, whose head hung down.

"We did it!" I whooped, exultant, and clapped him across the back. "Damn!"

He looked slowly up into my eyes. Paul's face was ravaged and old. He tried to speak but no words came out. Instead a dry sob rose up from deep inside him, and then he began to howl and shake. His wailing was primeval as the fire itself, primeval as murder.

I pulled him close to me, smelling him as we hugged, feeling his beard scratchy against my stubble.

Eleven

In my dream my mother wanted me to drink my milk and I wanted to climb into her lap and bury my face in her neck; she said no, I had to drink my milk first. I was miserably sad at being unable to hug my mother, it seemed entirely cruel and unaccountable. She understood how I felt and looked sad herself, but couldn't let on whatever was really happening. Something horrible and terrifying was preventing her from showing what she really felt. She shook her head sadly, denying me the comfort of her lap. "What have you been doing to yourself?" she said. I was flooded with guilt and jerked awake.

A voice was saying, "My God you look like death warmed over." It sounded exactly like Paul's mother, Estelle. "Death warmed over" was one of many arrows in her quiver of pointed observations you just might have heard somewhere else.

Estelle here? I couldn't incorporate. This whole thing was reaching my brain through the haze of too little sleep, and the alarm of being awakened by my troubling dream. But I couldn't help myself, I began to laugh. Estelle in Scottsburg was every bit as incongruous as Nixon on the beach in San Clemente in his wool suit and black shoes.

Estelle turned to where I had flopped on the couch with a sleeping bag when we had returned from the fire line. "Thank God you've arrived safely, Estelle," I said, furry-mouthed. "We've done nothing but worry about you."

She wanted to frown at my impudence but couldn't help being pleased, and smiled instead. Estelle's smile was one of the world's great smiles, a moon of kindly pleasure I always did my best to tickle into view. Then a dark thought crossed her mind, and she turned sternly back toward her son.

At seeing his mother appear in the doorway, followed by a man holding two bags and a makeup kit, Paul had yelped, "Ma?" Then he froze, and hadn't moved or spoken since.

"Ma?" he said now. "What the hell . . . Ma?"

"Oh, Lollipop," she cried, and rushed to him, grasping him in an enveloping hug and rocking him against her pillowy chest. Not to put too fine a point on it, Estelle was *zaftig*. She carried herself jauntily and I had once heard her late husband describe her as having, "a fine hitch in her gitalong."

Paulie seemed to shrink within her grasp and hang there like a rag doll. I knew that when she was finished with Paul, I was next. As fast as I could I threw back the sleeping bag and like the coward I am started toward the blessed privacy of the bathroom. The bare floor was cold.

"Where do I put these?" the driver asked me as I passed.

"Anywhere."

"You the one supposed to have murdered that guy?"

"No," I said. "Him. Lollipop."

"Huh. I have to head back to town now," he said. "My day man is due in a couple of hours and they'll bust my chops, you know? If I'm late. But the lady needed a ride, right? What could I do? She told me about the murder and everything when I picked her up at the airport. So."

At the airport? I looked closely and sure enough this guy was wearing a city taxi badge. Estelle had taken a 120 mile cab ride. Unbelievable. I did a quick calculation—my mind slip-ping into taxi gear even though it had been some time since I had driven myself—and came up with $350. The best ride of his life.

"So I got to head back now," he said.

"Lollipop'll take care of you," I said, nearly running into the bathroom where I closed the door behind me and began to laugh so convulsively I had to slide down onto the cold tiles and wrap my arms around myself to stop. Then I lost it again while I was brushing my teeth and swallowed a glob of Crest.

I reopened the cut under my ear while I was shaving and the blood looked like strawberry ripple oozing into the white shaving cream. The silent Italian strikes again. I stuck a tiny piece of toilet paper on the cut to stop its bleeding. I was thinking that the first thing I wanted to get done today was to find this Peyton character. There was more to talk about with Annie Bayard, too. I wanted to call Jake Braunstein but that would wait until later in the afternoon when he was back from court; there's no point in calling a litigator before 4 p.m. unless it happens to be the judge's afternoon for golf. I should check in with Peter at my answering service. I wondered if I would run into Lil.

When I had shaved, showered, dried myself slowly, combed my hair, and even rinsed the sink and shower, in short, when I had done everything I could to delay my return to the enactment of mother and son reunited, I wiped that grin right off my face and marched myself back inside.

The cabdriver was gone, having left Estelle's bags just inside the door. They were matching powder-blue Naugahyde with wide straps and big shiny buckles. Estelle was in the kitchen peering into a cabinet, one hand still holding the cabinet door open, the other adjusting her glasses so she could peer over them. Her mascara was smudged, and Paul's face was still fire smudged. They looked like they were related.

"You're sure you don't keep them somewhere else?" she asked.

"I know what I've got and don't have, Ma."

"You really should you know, teabags, graham crackers, things that won't go bad if you have an emergency."

"I've *got* an emergency," Paul said. "And I don't have any teabags. For God's sake, Ma."

"Aha!" Estelle said, having spotted me. "Another precinct heard from. You don't look so pale and sick now that you've shaved and cleaned up. There's no teabags," she told me. "Okay, when in Rome, I'll drink coffee. If I don't sleep, I don't sleep."

"You know, Estelle," I said, "I think you must have lost some weight, you look great."

"Mr. Ha-Ha," she said, shrewdly. "You know what I think? I think when people can't tell you how young you look anymore what they tell you instead is, 'Estelle, you look great.' " She spread her plump arms wide. "I don't get a hug?"

I gave myself up to the scents of talc, Tabú, tic tacs, and Estelle's warmth.

"You're crazy, Estelle," I said at the end of the clinch. "You know that?"

"Who wouldn't be?" she asked rhetorically. "I'll make us all some coffee and then I want to know exactly what's happening. From both of you. I suppose there's nothing a person could eat for breakfast?"

I snapped my fingers. "That's what we forgot," I said to Paul. "The supermarket shop." He nodded absently. Paul was still wrung dry by last night's frightful effort and release. The lights were on but nobody was home. Seeing this, Estelle's tone and mood shifted dramatically.

"I couldn't sit there in Chicago and not know," she said. "You do understand, don't you, Paul?"

Paul went over to her and taking her shoulders in his hands kissed her on the cheek. She took hold of his bicep and kneaded it in her hands, continuing long after he had released her. I could see it made him uncomfortable.

"Now," she finally said with a long sigh, and busied herself making coffee. "How long has this been around?" She lifted the tin of evaporated milk gingerly with her fingers.

"It's okay," Paul said.

"I'll start a shopping list," she said. "Maybe one of you boys can drive me into town later. No rush."

We drank our coffee and munched toast while Paul and I gave Estelle the *Reader's Digest* condensed version of what had been happening. I assured her that Braunstein was a very good lawyer.

"Because," Estelle said, "we must get the very, very best person for Paul with this awful thing. Money doesn't come into it."

"Well," I said finally, pushing away from the table, "I've got things to do."

"You go right ahead with your plans," Estelle said. "I'm not going to get in anybody's way. I thought I'd just clean up a little around here and take a bath. The shopping can wait."

I shrugged into my windbreaker and filled my pockets with keys, cigars, money, a handkerchief, my pad and pen. I owned a pistol but never took it out of the closet. Maybe because I had been a reporter my pen and pad were the weapons I took with me into the daily fray.

"I'll walk you out," Paul said.

When we turned the corner of the house and were out of Estelle's sight I began to laugh again but Paul managed only a tense, wan smile. After all, she was *his* mother. My heart was pierced by a sharp sadness as I remembered my dream.

"You okay?" I asked. "After last night and everything?"

"Yeah," he said. "It was a huge relief, you know? I hadn't lost control completely like that since I was a kid. Just everything went whoosh."

"I know."

"The air feels moist, I think the fog's in. It's hard to be sure with all this smoke still. But I think I'm safe now, the house I mean."

"God, I don't know the last time I worked that hard for that long," I said, rolling my stiff shoulders, then stretching my back like a cat.

"You know what the taxi cost her?" Paul asked.

"How much?"

"Over three hundred bucks."

Meter, meter on the wall. "She should have rented a car, it would have saved her a lot of money."

"She doesn't like to drive in the dark on unfamiliar roads. Where are you running off to, you coward?"

"Bad words, Lollipop." That got an abashed smile. "I'm going to find Peyton."

"Try the Hanna place first," Paul said. "He hangs around there a lot."

"I will."

"You better take mine," he said, meaning his bright red Bronco. "You'll rip the bottom of your car to shreds on these roads. Man," he laughed, "Bunko's scored himself a Caddy-lak."

Now it was my turn to be abashed. "Girls like it," I said. "What if you need to get somewhere?"

"Well, I'm going to make some phone calls, check on the fire, and get the forecast and stuff. I'll be okay. To tell you the truth, I feel best about staying near the house today. You know?"

"Sure."

Down by the creek the only sign of the fire crew that had been there to defend the house was the debris they had left behind, Coke cans and butts and the like.

"Give Estelle a broom and set her to work," I said.

Paul tossed me his keys and I climbed into the Bronco. "It's a long way above the ground," I said from the driver's seat, as I began to locate and identify the various switches, buttons, and levers.

Paul swung the door shut with both hands and leaned on the open window frame. "Hey, were you and Lil crossing wrists there or what?"

"Hey," I said happily. "Hey."

Twelve

I found Annie Bayard first. She was crossing the road on horseback where the packed earth leveled out into the county-maintained road a stone's throw above Scottsburg "center." Everything was exactly as it had been the last time I was downtown, including a gray Eisenhower era van that I saw wasn't an indisposed vehicle so much as a piece of public statuary.

Annie reined in her mount when I hailed her, but her face didn't betray any pleasure in meeting me again. It was a peasant's face, pretty enough, with broad, high cheekbones and rosy spots in both cheeks. Her name was French but she made me think of the Bohemians I had known around Chicago with names like Schmid and Fiala and natures as thick as porridge. She didn't dismount and she didn't say anything, just sat in her saddle eyeing me mistrustfully.

So I dismounted, climbing out of the Bronco, and walked toward her. I stopped at her boots. "Guys my height aren't used to looking up at people they're talking to," I said.

It didn't exactly charm her; I wasn't flashed a won-over smile, but at least she did swing down from the saddle, making it clear all the while that this interlude wasn't going to be the highlight of her morning. She had on leather gloves and chaps fastened over her jeans. Her bandana was emerald green.

"I don't have more than a minute," she said. "One of our old ladies hasn't come down to the corral." She looked at her watch. "And I have to be back home before Eve's due for her next shot."

"Laetrile, right? From the pits of plums, isn't it?"

"Apricots."

"You think it's medically sound? Don't some people say it's quackery, that any improvement is brought about by a placebo effect?"

"Doctors don't like what they don't control," she said dryly. "That's a subject I know a whole lot about."

"Right, from when you were a nurse. Listen, Annie. I want to explain what I'm doing. Paul is my friend and all, but this, what I'm doing, is my job. Asking the kinds of questions people sometimes are reluctant to answer. You understand?"

"Like I told you before, whyn't you stop bullshitting and just get on to what's on your mind?"

You meet people sometimes with whom you just couldn't be friendly, the prickly unease was built into the first look you exchanged and even if you were both polite as could be, you would always be fencing and stumbling over each other. That's how it was with Annie Bayard, except she didn't bother to be polite and I was elaborately indirect.

"Okay, it's personal. I heard that you had an abortion and that Rich Hanna was, uh . . ." I was trying to think of some word beside father.

"Who told you that?" Her eyes blazed and she clenched her gloved fists against her thighs. The color in her cheeks flamed.

An old green Chevy flatbed with a plank for a front bumper came rattling past us and the driver tapped his horn in greeting. I didn't recognize him but I suppose Annie did. The interruption was propitious, though, because it broke a spell of impending violence. I had thought she might take a swing at me for a second there.

"It doesn't matter who told me, does it?" I said. "I mean, everybody around here knows everybody else's business, just like anyplace. Lots of people could have told me. I guess the point is what happened with you and Rich."

"Rich is dead," she said. As she was saying that she understood it was the point exactly: Rich was dead. "What happened, and I'm not saying it did, it ain't no business of yours."

She lacked conviction, so I waited. So did she. I outwaited her.

"I'm thirty-eight years old," she finally said, looking furiously into my face. "I was raised a good Catholic, he didn't want to admit it was his, even after I explained how we could take a blood test and everything. It didn't matter, I was wasting my breath, he didn't want any part of a child. That's when I did what had to be done. Is that what you wanted to hear?" she practically shouted.

"Annie," I said, "When Sheriff Etter gets around to start questioning people about Rich's death he's going to ask you where you were on the morning he was murdered."

I could have sworn that what showed briefly in her eyes was fear of being found out. "Will you leave me alone?" she asked shrilly. She lifted the pointy toe of her boot back into a stirrup and mounted her gray mare in one fluid motion. "Will you jus' please leave us all alone? You got no call doing this to us." She made a chucking sound and dug her spurs into the horse's flanks. It took off at a fast trot, its hooves clattering on the hard-packed earth.

I watched her ride up into the forest until she was obscured by the smoke and deep darkness in the forest even at midday. Lost Sam was still burning nearby and though Scottsburg wasn't under immediate threat it wasn't out of danger yet either. I continued toward the Hanna Ranch thinking that it was time to find out more about Annie Bayard and that maybe the place to start was in San Jose, at Valley Medical Center where she had worked until Roy Hanna hired her away to look after his ailing wife. And him?

I left Paul's Bronco at the roadside and trudged into the

Hanna clan's open-air living room. Today washing was strung on a long line between two trees, mostly kids' clothes and some men's shirts and underwear. The shirts were worn so thin from repeated washings you could see through them. I saw two mothers looking after infants, and older kids running in a pack playing some game. The retriever was curled up in the dust at his master's feet, with its snout tucked under its tail.

"Cut yourself shavin'," Roy said by way of greeting. He was in a lawn chair, his short bowed legs crossed at the ankles, fiddling with a bridle in his lap.

I pulled the scrap of toilet tissue loose. I had forgotten all about it and it had stuck to the cut as the blood dried. It stung when it came loose.

"I had the first barbershop shave of my life up in San Francisco a few days ago and my face hasn't felt right since," I said, running a hand over my cheek.

"You ever wonder how a blind man feels when he's shaving?" Roy asked.

I sat down in an empty chair. "I never have," I said. The only person sitting with Roy this morning was a pudgy boy of fifteen or sixteen.

"Mornin', Mr. Henry," the boy said politely. I was surprised he knew my name, it made me aware that I was being talked about.

"Used to wonder about that," Roy said. "So then I tried onc't myself. You wobble a blame sight mor'n when you're camping and don't have no mirror, your hand ain't so steady, leastways mine wasn't. I kept my eyes closed until I was finished, like a blind man has to." He laughed. "Whoo boy, I was a sorry sight, I cut myself a face that looked like a cattle guard."

I laughed, impressed. "That's a real commitment to finding something out for its own sake, Roy."

"W'all," Roy drawled. "I don't know about that, blind man's committed, I was jus' doin' an experiment."

"What's the difference, grandpa?" the boy asked.

"It's like ham an' eggs, you see?" Roy said. "Chicken's involved, sure, but the pig is committed."

Not so different, I thought, from me dropping into the midst of their community only to turn around and leave when my questions were answered. I wondered if Roy Hanna was that subtle.

Roy spat against the smoldering ash can, raising a hiss. "Sorry we cain't offer you nuthin' today," he said. "Eve's not herself, she's in, restin'." Clearly he didn't want me to linger and I had no wish to impose.

"I was looking for Peyton," I said, standing. "Any idea where I might find him?"

Tommy piped up, "I could show you."

"Tha's good," Roy said. "You go on ahead with Tommy here."

Thirteen

"You a detective?" Tommy asked. There was awe in the question. We were crawling uphill behind a couple of water tankers and a transport. The air was thin enough for my ears to have begun to plug up, so we must have been at several thousand feet at least, and the valley fell away dramatically although the smoke was too thick for much visibility.

"Yep," I said.

Tommy was about fifteen or sixteen, overweight, wearing the same sort of getup as the men: a worn shirt with rhinestone snaps, jeans, boots, and a ten-gallon chocolate-colored hat with a high crown.

"You ever meet that Spenser?" he asked.

For a moment I was flabbergasted. But of course he knew Spenser from the television show and not the books; that a boy his age was unable to distinguish between real people and television tales wasn't entirely unexpected. After all, he'd grown up in Ronald Reagan's make-believe America.

"Never had that pleasure," I told him. "He's out of Boston, I'm based in Frisco."

He nodded solemnly and we rode on for a moment in silence. "I think Hawk can take him," Tommy said.

I was trying to think of how best to respond, whether to fall in with him or not, when he mooted my decision.

"There," he said, pointing a pudgy index finger.

A dirt track led through a stand of ghostly, ash-dusted trees. I followed the track until we emerged in a clearing. There was a two-story cabin, a barn and paddock, and the usual array of trucks, cars, and tractors, including a white Ford pickup mounted on blocks that was being stripped for parts. What made Peyton's spread distinctive, though, was an Indian teepee and some kind of bunker built of what looked like close-packed mud.

Tommy was out of the Bronco and on the ground before I had the emergency brake set. "I'll git 'im," he said, half-running, half-walking toward the door of the house. He was eager to please.

I leaned against the fender, waiting. The fire was close and the heat dense. In fact I could see an isolated burn in the distance licking at a fir tree. I rubbed the toe of one of my city boots, made in Italy not Austin, against the back of my jeans leg to wipe away the dust and ash. Peyton came through the open door at just that moment, catching me at what I felt to be an effete gesture. Real men only cleaned their boots on Saturday night. He didn't appear to react.

Peyton was again dressed all in black from his ten-gallon hat like Tommy's to boots that were some kind of reptile skin. The top three buttons of his shirt were open showing a hairless chest and a stomach with ridges of muscle. He was almost my height, a few inches more than six feet, wide through the shoulders and narrow through the hips. He had slightly slanted eyes and bad teeth.

"What?" he said, when he had reached me.

"My name is Henry," I said, offering Peyton no more names than he had, so far as I knew. "I'm investigating the death of Rich Hanna. I understand he was a neighbor of yours."

He motioned beyond a stand of madrone trees. "Over there," he said. "You have the wrong place."

"It's you I'd like to talk to."

"You work for Paul Richards, who killed him." It was a statement of fact. I kept quiet, not wanting to begin by disagreeing.

"For his lawyer," I said. "I was told that you knew this area better than most. I was also told that Rich cheated you. I thought maybe you could help me understand what went down." The combination of stroking his vanity while appealing to the aggrieved part of his nature sprung his lock, as it almost always will.

"He tried," Peyton said. "We'll talk in the Round House." Tommy had wandered away and left us alone. He turned and led the way toward the mound like a man-size anthill.

"Fire's close," I said conversationally.

"The Bigs ordered us out," Peyton answered, shrugging.

At the mound, three crude steps led below the earth's surface and into the dark cavern below. He faced me.

"I am Esalen," he said. "Our church is outside, the sky is our roof, the mountains are our altars, Mother Earth is our floor. This is a ceremonial house, Round House, that we use for teaching." Then he descended.

Both of us had to bend almost double to make it inside the Round House, where a section of the earth floor was covered in clean gravel. Thick bent poles supported the wattle roof. Tom-toms, ceremonial sticks with animal faces carved into them, dried white bones, feathers and bead headdresses hung from pegs or were placed in crevices in the walls. Peyton sat on a brightly colored cushion and braced his back against the wall with his boots extended toward the center poles, where a stove also had been placed. The stone was cold. He gestured for me to take the cushion next to his.

"I have all kind of medicines in here," he said. "This one is wild celery root that we use in healing." He cut a short section of the root with a Bowie knife he took from a sheath on his belt, and held the celery under my nose to smell it.

Then he took a pestle and began to grind the root. "I teach people. Many, many people are coming to learn because they're ready to come back into harmony and balance with Mother Earth. We are killing the earth; Mother Earth is a living organism, she's alive, she breathes.

"This fire was prophesied, you know. In ancient times they predicted a time of flood and fire. The flood's been happening in Arizona and New Mexico, did you know that? They never hardly get any rain and it's rained forty, fifty inches down there. And we should be getting that here and we're not, the weather is going around us."

He laid the mortar and pestle aside and began to beat rhythmically on a tom-tom. After a moment, he chanted. I listened to his incomprehensible wailing call, mentally drumming my fingers. He must have sensed my impatience because he stopped with the tom-tom and looked at me inquisitively.

"I heard," I said, "that you and Rich had a property line disagreement, that he was trying to take some of your land." It was the tradition of my people to seize our chance to talk when it presented itself.

"Everything today is based on money," Peyton said. "Money's become the 'spirituality' of life, they forgot about the earth. Rich was greedy for more than he had, that's why he wanted to steal my land. That's why he planted marijuana. He wanted more, more, more; he wasn't satisfied with all that Mother Earth provided."

The celery smell mingled with the cold ashes in the stove.

"Did you have to take him to court in order to stop him?" I asked.

He nodded. "We were supposed to have a hearing next month; he made his lawyer delay until he had time to harvest his crop before anybody from the court came out to survey our claims. He was very angry."

"I suppose from everything I've heard about him that he probably threatened you, too."

"Many, many times."

"What did he threaten to do?"

"Carve me a new asshole." Peyton smiled, showing his brown teeth. "Let me see, use me for bear bait. He was a tongue-tied man but when he was threatening his tongue became loose." What Peyton was telling me about Rich would fit right into the self-defense theory Braunstein wanted to construct for Paul. "He wanted to kill me," Peyton said, and resumed his soft pounding of the tom-tom.

"What did you do about that, him wanting to kill you?"

He smiled enigmatically and kept up his tom-toming.

"In nature," he finally said, closing his eyes, "everything was once in balance. The coyote and all the wild animals, they take care of themselves. But there's no predator for man."

"Except man."

"Except man," he echoed.

"So the question is, did you kill Rich Hanna?"

He opened his eyes. Even in the near dark of the Round House I could see he was amused.

"That's a stupid question," Peyton said.

"It may be. But I find that stupidity sometimes works where cleverness fails."

"Rock smashes scissors," he said.

"We all play our games. You brought me down here because this is where you are the strongest, where you felt the safest and most protected from my questions."

"So you asked your strongest question," he said. "To test my protection. And what has it got for you? Ambiguity? More suspicion?"

"I've been told that you didn't always follow Esalen ways."

"No, I had a vision when I was eight years old. I didn't understand what it was, it was a vision about these mountains and it scared hell out of me. I had another vision when I was thirteen. Traditionally the young people who were the spiritual leaders would have an old teacher to go and ask. My Indian grandfather was dead. My father, he didn't understand. I was very confused but I spent time alone in these mountains and I learned what the Ventana had to teach me. I found some of the caves that my ancestors lived in, I found paintings of little children, and hand prints of my ancestors. I put my hand against theirs and they spoke to me without words. There are no words to explain what I felt in that cave.

"This Ventana is a gateway, it's an ancient prophecy, six thousand years old. In Spanish *ventana* means window, the Spaniards took the name from the Esalen people. We believe that when you die your spirit goes right out that window, it goes right up the Carmel River and goes out. The Ventana is an exit, an exit for souls." He began to pound his tom-tom, closing his eyes and chanting with his head thrown back.

When he finished he got to his feet and led the way out crablike, since neither of us could stand upright. I was happy to be in the open air and unconfined, the Round House had been dark and claustrophobic. Yet, strangely, I felt something powerful receding from me, some spirit or power that had been within. Peyton started back toward his log house, walking slowly so we could continue to talk.

"Did Rich harvest his crop before he was killed?" I asked.

He smiled, narrowing his eyes to slits. "Yes, a bumper crop. He went to San Francisco and sold it a couple of days before he was killed. It is a good cash crop in time of drought, once it is germinated it will grow even if it is thirsty."

"And the property line dispute?"

"We have agreed, his lawyer and I, to resolve it in the spirit of this land. I am negotiating to purchase his property from his estate. It is very complicated because he died intestate.

"See? You have learned more than you expected, coming here. You felt the power of the Round House and the sadness of leaving it, I felt your regret. Before you go, come inside with me and I will enter your name and address in my computer files, that way you will receive our newsletter, someday you will return and ride with us into the wilderness. The sweat lodge weekend package is cleansing and affordable."

Fourteen

Peyton hadn't bothered to actually deny killing Rich Hanna, and so the Esalen medicine man went on the short list along with the cowgirl. I felt as if I were lost in a Luke Short novel, a country-mile wide of my element. Young Tommy Garber respected my ruminative mood and kept his mouth shut on the way back down to where I dropped him near the Hanna place.

"Thanks, Mr. Henry," he said.

"Hey, pal, thank you for showing me where to find Peyton. It was a help."

A wonderfully ingenuous smile lit up his coarse-skinned moon face. "Really?"

"Really, no kidding."

"Shoot," he said bashfully. "Mr. Henry?"

"What is it, Tommy?"

"Can I help you again sometime?"

"Absolutely. Listen, I can trust you, can't I?" I looked around as if to see if we were being overheard and dropped my voice confidentially.

"Yes, sir."

"All right, now here's what I need. I want you to keep your eyes open and report to me anything suspicious, okay? I'm kind of deputizing you, but it's got to be strictly on the QT."

I saw the question wash over his unguarded face. Oh God, fifteen was so many poor answers ago I had forgotten most of the questions. "Secret, just between us," I explained.

"You mean like any suspicious gangsters?" he said hesitantly. "Right?"

"That's the idea, or anything you hear. Keep your ear to the ground. I need you to be my eyes and ears, you see?"

"Yes, sir."

"Okay, then. I'll want a report the next time I see you."

"Yes, sir."

I put a cautionary finger to my lips. "Don't forget, strictly on the QT."

He imitated my gesture. "QT," he said.

I waved and pulled away. In my rearview I saw Tommy turn and tear up the drive to the Hanna place. He would, I knew, uncover a plague of suspicious gangsters such as peopled the dreams of Elliot Ness. A sweet, polite, unsophisticated kid.

Paul was at the dining room table reading the *Chicago Trib.* "You find Peyton?" he asked, putting the paper down when I came in.

"Is he for real, or what?"

"You mean the *I am Esalen* stuff?"

"The sky is my roof, yeah."

"There's a difference of opinion locally," Paul said. "Personally I think he's sincere. But maybe a little simplistic."

"Would it be racist to say that I found him to be a cunning redskin?"

"Yes," Paul said, "it sure would."

"Okay then, I think he enjoys being an enigma, figures on making a lot of money, and has a high tolerance for risk. He did tell me that Rich Hanna was growing dope. Is that generally known?"

"I think I'd heard that before. A few people around here do, it's a way of making ends meet. It's a different scene from up in Humboldt though, no punji sticks or guns. Well, every-body around here is armed and naturally that includes the growers, but I'd be surprised if there were any Uzis. It's more of a laid-back, sixties kind of scene.

"By the way, Jake Braunstein called while you were gone," he said. "There's a hearing set for the week after next, I have to be there. He wants you to give him a call, too."

"Okay, I was going to anyway. What's new with the fire?"

"The wind's out of the north, right in its face, and the humidity's up a bit, too. They're predicting heavy fog tonight, so I'd say the only real threat now is to the homes up along Anastasia Ridge. They're predicting containment within thirty-six hours."

"Good," I said, half-listening. "Where's Estelle?"

Paul tilted his head toward the stairs leading down to his bedroom. "Resting. Bunko, do you think Peyton may really have killed Rich?"

"I don't know, but it's certainly possible. Did you know he's negotiating to buy Rich's property from the estate? And he says Rich was threatening to kill him because of their property-line dispute. I asked him outright."

"If he killed Rich?" Paul sounded incredulous. "What did he say?"

"That it was a stupid question."

"Jeez." There was doubt in Paul's eyes, doubt about me, not Peyton.

"Paulie, I just had an instinct that it was the right question at that moment. And I did get some interesting information as a result because he didn't bother to deny it."

"What does that mean?"

"I'm not sure. Maybe that he wanted to lead me on, or that his guilt got in the way, or that it didn't seem necessary."

"How does that help, I don't follow?"

"Specifically? I don't really know, but it raises enough other questions so that I'll keep poking around Peyton."

"It's interesting, the way you work. There's a lot of trial and error, and you have to be comfortable with ambiguity."

"Thesis and antithesis is my middle name, pally. Listen, I'm going up to San Jose tomorrow, there's some stuff about Annie Bayard I want to check out there."

"Annie?"

"If Peyton's the thesis, she's the antithesis. You mind if I use the phone to call the city? I'll put it on the credit card."

"Don't do that, just make your calls. I'm going to take a walk." Paul got up. "I feel like what I'm accused of really hasn't sunk in yet, I mean even though I was in the jail. I *know* all this is happening but I'm puzzled by my own reactions, I seem so distant from any feeling about it. Except I get really scared every once in awhile. The nights have been pretty bad. I feel like I'm not sure what I really know anymore. Do you ever feel that way?"

"Yeah," I said. "More than I admit. I think it's smarter to admit how little you know, and how confused you are, than to try and pretend."

"And that works?"

"Not usually," I said.

We both laughed. "Make your phone calls," he said, and headed out. I sat on a high stool beside the wall-mounted phone and dialed my own number in San Francisco. Peter picked up at the answering service on the third ring.

"Ben Henry's line."

"It's me, Peter."

"Oh, Be-en," Peter said, cramming two syllables into the three letters of my name in his uniquely Belgian way. "I am on another line, I will shoot right back to you."

" 'Kay." I listened to the long-distance hum.

"Be-en, I'm sorry to delay you. I've been worried, how is your friend?"

"My friend? You mean Paul? He's fine, but how did you know about that? I don't remember saying anything before I came down here about why I was coming."

"No, Giselle in Mr. Braunstein's office was telling me about the terrible accusations against him. She called only an hour ago, Mr. Braunstein wanted to hear from you."

"Okay, anything else?"

"No, Be-en, that is all of it taken care of."

"Okay, Peter. I'm still at this same number, the one I left with you."

"I have it right here, Be-en. Tell your friend how I am sorry for his troubles. It is a great help, to know people are pulling on the rope for you when there is trouble."

Fifteen

Lil had come around to make us a hot supper; she thought we were probably tired of eating out of cans. Paul, meanwhile, returned, only to leave again. He took the Bronco into Carmel Valley village to fill its tank, pick up his mail at his post office box, and run other errands that had been neglected.

Being left alone with Lil was in no way objectionable. She had brought round a bunch of stuff from her garden, ripe irregularly shaped tomatoes, yellow squash, waxy green peppers, onions, and a glossy purple eggplant, as well as a container full of raspberries.

"I wouldn't mind a drink while I work," she said. "Got a beer cold?"

I found three bottles of Spaten Munich in the fridge. Then I began to look for a church key at the same time Lil was pulling open drawers looking for something she needed, too, and our hips bumped. Neither of us moved away at once. No matter how many times it happens, the electric softness of touching a woman for the first time brings a jolt of shocked recognition.

She stepped back. "You've got an admirer here, you know."

"I do?" It came out as a croak.

She laughed and danced away, a bone-handled knife in her large, capable hand. "Tommy Garber talks about you as if you were a Masked Stranger."

"He's a nice kid," I said, trying to recover my composure. "Has he got some sort of problem? I mean he looks sixteen but he acts like he's eight or nine."

"He's backward," Lil said, starting to slice the green pepper on a cutting board built into the countertop beneath a kitchen window. "But he's awfully helpful and loyal. He's a little in love with me. Boys his age have a habit of falling in love with blond hair and a friendly smile."

"Boys of every age have been known to do that," I said.

"There's something I want to ask you," she said, dicing the pepper with deft strokes.

"Try me." Please.

"What I want to know is, are you going to open those beers?"

I blushed and she laughed at me. I found the church key and put her bottle open on the counter beside her.

"I deputized him."

"He told me, he's thrilled." She began to peel an onion, sniffling and dabbing at her eyes with the back of her wrist. I watched her, concentrating on the long line of her narrow waist. She put the knife down and took a swallow of beer.

I took a sip of mine. "He told me he'd watch out for suspicious gangsters." As I said it, some thought itching to be born tickled the back of my mind. I was trying to scratch it mentally, looking for the prize underneath like a lottery ticket, when I heard footsteps on the stairs. Estelle. I had forgotten all about her.

"Morning," I said, turning to greet her as she tromped heavily upstairs. "You're in time for supper."

"Hello, Ben dear," she said drowsily. "It must be jet lag, I never nap but I fell right off. Hello?" she said to Lil.

"Hi. You're Paul's mother."

"Yes, Estelle Richards."

"I'm Lil Palmer."

"I had an aunt in Evanston named Lillian, may she rest in peace. It's such a lovely name."

"It is," Lil agreed. "I'm a Lily. There's something kind of cloying about Lily, don't you think?"

"Not at all, not in the least," Estelle said. "Like *Lilies of the Field*, that lovely movie with Sydney Poitier."

"Well, anyway," Lil said. "I think it's wonderful you came all the way out here. We're all very sorry about what's happened to Paul. The sheriff's made an awful mistake but I'm sure it'll be straightened out before too long."

Estelle nodded, and her eyes, puffy with sleep, suddenly were brimming with tears. Apprehensively she asked, "Where is Paul?"

"He's gone into town," I told her. "Lil brought round some vegetables and stuff she grew to make us supper."

"Can I help?" Estelle asked. She was wearing a flowing dressing gown, a muumuu, with a pattern of pink, red, and purple flowers. She peered over her glasses at what Lil was cooking. "What gorgeous tomatoes," Estelle exclaimed. "You can't find them like that in a market."

"Want to blanch them?"

"I'd love to," Estelle said. She went without hesitation to the proper cabinet and brought out a large saucepan that she filled from the tap. After she put the water on to boil she splayed her fingers and peered at them intently, sighing. "My nails are a mess," she said. They looked long enough and red enough to me, but what did I know about it?

"Excuse me," Estelle said. "I'll just be a minute, I just want to freshen up and throw some clothes on." As she turned to go back downstairs she caught my eye and raised an inquisitive eyebrow. Lil had resumed slicing with her back to us.

Estelle mouthed something I couldn't make out.

"What?" I asked silently.

"Is—she—Paul's—girl?"

I shook my head no. A voice inside me said: no, mine if I'm lucky. I flushed with a feeling of disloyalty to Jessica Gage.

"She's—beautiful," Estelle mouthed before she went downstairs again.

There was a silence after she departed. Then Lil said, "What a nice thing for her to say." She turned her head and smiled at me with a private amusement.

Sixteen

A bird chittering at first light woke me with suspicious gang-sters on my mind. More particularly, a suspicious gangster named Dink Ebhardt who operated a marijuana supermarket in the Haight Ashbury. It was Dink's name under the scratch-off obstruction my mind had tossed up when I had been deputizing Tommy Garber. Dink went all the way back to the beginning of time, that is to say the year before the Summer of Love, and knew everything about, and everybody in, the dope trade. Dink was white and he was twenty-one-plus but it was Braunstein who kept him free despite the persistent efforts of the SFPD narcotics unit to remedy that situation. If Rich Hanna had recently sold his crop in San Francisco the chances were good that the Dinker would either have bought it himself, or else would know somebody who knew some-body who knew something.

By now I was wide awake. There was no reason not to be on my way to San Jose to find out what I could about Annie Bayard. It was surprisingly cold in the house this morning. I was just starting out the door when Paul, who was curled up in a sleeping bag on the floor beside the couch, mumbled,

"Don't forget your hat." I wasn't sure whether he was talking in his sleep or making a feeble joke. Maybe in Paul's sleeping mind my thinking about Dink had connected up with Roy Hanna's remark that he always forgot his hat when he smoked marijuana. Things like that are always happening.

I settled myself in the extrawide, deeply padded seat of the Cadillac and inhaled the leather aroma. It felt like home in a funny way: what I wanted from a car was a living room on wheels, something comfy and very little trouble to drive, a secure place for my coffee, firm lower back support, in sum an insulated place where I could smoke and think with a mini-. mum of interruption. The windshield wipers succeeded in doing very little but streak the dust and ash on the window, and the radio picked up nothing but static.

As I was locking the gate, a white Toyota pickup whipped by at a good clip heading up into the wilderness fire area. Roy Hanna was in the cab of the truck wedged between Roy, Jr., at the wheel and Annie Bayard. There were two rifles mounted on the rack. I didn't think the Hanna clan was off to hunt boar or lion, and the afterimage of their determined faces sent me following after them. Something was up.

The four-wheel drive Toyota was moving too fast for me to catch up, but they were easy to follow because at this early hour it was the only vehicle moving on the unpaved road, and it left a trail of amber dust swirling in its wake. The sun wasn't visible at all and the time could have been 5 A.M. or 8 A.M. but in fact was a few minutes after six.

I followed the dust trail onto one of those horse tracks that everybody in Scottsburg knew and used. I had to get out of the car to open a wooden swinging gate, and then inch the car along to avoid scraping the bottom, and the engine sputtered once. When I got back to town the air filter would have to be changed. I kept climbing and climbing through dense, un-burned forest until finally I went through a stand of mossy old oaks to where the track ended at the edge of a large, bowl-shaped meadow. What I saw there made me climb out.

A line of bulldozers was drawn up along one perimeter of

what I realized must be Hanna Meadow. The engine of the large, blunt machines were muttering and clanking menacingly. Drawn up beside the dozers were two small trucks with official insignias on their doors. Several men in khaki uniforms were standing over a map spread out on the hood of one truck, but none of the men was looking down at it.

Instead they were staring at the Hannas. The white Toyota was facing them head-on, both its doors akimbo. Annie stood a short distance off to the side. Roy and Roy, Jr., looked insubstantial beside the mechanical behemoths and the small army of rangers and drivers they were facing across maybe fifty feet, but the rifles the Hanna men held cradled across their arms seemed to even things out.

I kept walking closer until Roy, Jr., shifted his weight fractionally in my direction and I stopped, obeying his unspoken command. Roy, Jr., never took his eyes off the rangers, nor did his father. At that moment the old man looked as deadly as the boar he hunted.

"Don't give a damn 'bout no orders, Gordy. I'll shoot the first man who comes onto my meadow," Roy said in a ringing voice.

"Roy, use some common sense, wontcha?" said the man addressed as Gordy. "You know me and I know you since Roy, Jr., here was a infant. Din't I save your place from fire back in sixty-four?"

"This ain't between you an' me, Gordy, and you know it, this's between them bureau-crats give you your orders. I cain't do nothing about the way they're destroyin' the forest and I cain't fight them taxin' me right out of existence but if one of your men tries to tear up this topsoil I wouldn't want to be him."

"You jus' take it easy now, Roy," said Gordy. He was in his ranger uniform with a yellow fire-retardant jacket unbuttoned over it. The idling nine-footers were making a godawful racket. The ashen face of the operator closest to Roy, a boy of perhaps nineteen, was a study in terror.

"You're the rancher, Roy," Gordy said. "I ain't goin' to do nothing without you say so."

"You're here without our say so," said Roy, Jr.

"Go cut your line somewhere where it won't kill more'n it saves," said old Roy, simply.

"Can't, Roy, like you said, got to follow my orders. Now listen here, I'm going to talk to them on the radio. I'll see what they say."

"Make it so it's clear to them, Gordy. I don't want to harm no man, you make it clear so they understand."

"I will, Roy." Gordy climbed into the truck and began a long palaver on his two-way. While he talked nothing moved, not the dozers, not the men. The fire was nowhere to be seen but its terrible destructive heat had us all frozen in place. Everybody and everything waited in silence for the decision of some boss down below at base camp who couldn't see the white fury and determination on the faces of Roy Hanna and his son.

"Okay, Roy," Gordy said when he finally was done on the radio. "How's about this, you bring your three-footer up here and widen this perimeter road? How's that strike you to do?"

"You going to clear those nines out of here?" asked Roy, Jr.

"Yes, I am, tha's exactly the thing I'm tellin' ya that Burress down there tole me. Burress got to have your word on widenin' the perimeter here so's he can authorize me to take my men 'round Anastasia Canyon. Cutting the line round Anastasia Canyon, tha's satisfactory with you, Roy?"

"We'll widen it," said Roy. The rifle was still in his arms and his face hadn't relented.

"I know you will, Roy," said Gordy. "And I'll do like I tole you, you know that too." He flapped his arms against his sides. "Damn, never been so glad for cold before in my entire life. Slowed this sucker right down."

"Jesus H. Christ," said Annie. It was as if her words were a collective sigh of relieved tension; suddenly men were talking again to each other and Gordy was pointing at his map and shouting orders. In a matter of minutes the dozers were clank-

ing into the woods and down into a canyon out of sight. It was
not yet 7 A.M.

"I'll get Scotty to bring that three-footer," Roy said to his
son. "You wait 'round."

Roy, Jr., nodded his assent. Annie glowered at me and
hopped in beside old Roy, who drove away without a word or
a look in my direction.

Roy, Jr., walked over to me. "Boy, you should not have
followed us up here. He wanted to take a shot at you back
there, we had to talk him out of it." He was smiling.

"You knew I was there? I must have been a mile behind
you."

"Oh, he knew, all right."

"What was this about?" I asked. "How'd you know they
were ready to dig a line across your meadow?"

"Fellow who drives for that boss Burress come and told us.
State boys like Gordy, they wanted to backburn the ridge
along Anastasia Canyon and save the meadow. Feds said no,
they were afraid the crew'd be caught between the two fires if
the wind shifted all of a sudden. Burress, he said he didn't give
a damn about the meadow. The fellow told us he said it had
sentimental value is all, and he was concerned more with life
and property."

"Man, it was a courageous thing you and your father did,
I'll tell you that."

"Courage doesn't have the least thing to do with it." He
offered me one of his cigarettes and we both lit up. Now that
things had quieted down I had a good look around the
meadow ringed by old oaks. It was by far the largest open
space I had seen in the forest, and it had a peacefulness that
only comes to some old places and a few old people.

"I got a thermos in the truck but it's gone back down with
them," Roy, Jr., said. "You know, they'll crush us Hannas
sooner or later, just like they crushed the Indians and the
Spaniards to take over this land in the first place."

"It's hard to imagine your dad crushed."

"No, not if he can fight what's crushing him. But you can't

fight against cancer, or taxes either for that matter. The whole damn place is up for sale anyway, it isn't going to be ours much longer. They taxed us right out of existence."

"You mean this meadow is for sale?"

"Hanna Ranch, every bit of it. We lost more money ranching than we ever knew we had, now we got a man over in Carmel who wants to break it into half-acre parcels and put vacation chalets on it. You can see all the way to Santa Cruz," he said, pointing, "when there ain't all this smoke."

"You'll sell?"

"If we didn't sell the Infernal Revenue's going to take it for taxes pretty soon, and this Lost Sam's burned up most of what else the family's got. Lost the house and everything."

I was confused. "You mean the trailer where your folks live?"

"No, the house," Roy said, shaking his head. "They don't live in the trailer, that's where me and my family stay. My father and mother live in the new house we built for them last year, up in Spiller Canyon. Burned down, let's see, four, no five days ago. Just damn lucky the insurance is all paid up."

"I didn't understand that," I said. "So, really, your dad was stopping them from churning up land that's going to be plowed under anyway for vacation houses?"

"This land was my great grandpa's," said Roy, Jr. "We'd have perished a long time ago without this meadow. Damn, I wish they hadn't taken that thermos, hot coffee'd hit the spot."

Seventeen

In the valley where silicon was king and the fog never reached, the temperature was pushing ninety at nine-thirty. In less time than it took to drive from New York to Philadelphia, I had passed through a succession of astoundingly different landscapes: from rugged wilderness, along the Pacific seacoast, across the Santa Cruz mountains, and finally into the hot, flat valley at the southern neck of San Francisco Bay where the twenty-first century was under creation.

What was remarkable, even more remarkable than the variety, beauty, and diversity of this corner of California, was how the longer you hung around the more habituated you became to what was all around you, bitching and moaning instead about crime, traffic, and parking problems. The parking lot at the South Hill medical complex was being torn up as part of a construction project, and I crawled along behind six or seven other cars looking for an empty stall that wasn't there to be found. Jackhammers were driving bolts into the girders of a new administration building, their noise as much a part of the therapeutic environment as syringes and bedpans. By the time I reached the hospital lobby the sun was glaring overhead and my shirt was sticking to my back.

South Hill smelled the way hospitals do, and made me grateful to be a stranger here. After several wrong turns as I picked my way through the maze of the hospital, I finally located Oncology on the sixth floor of the west wing. Its chief according to the nameplate outside his reception area was Dr. Bertrand Hammaker.

Dr. Hammaker's secretary was a middle-aged Chinese woman wearing a white blouse with a high, stiff collar that did an almost complete job of hiding the sag lines under her chin. Her stern expression didn't exactly melt into a warm smile of welcome when I explained I wanted just a moment of Dr. Hammaker's time in connection with a legal matter.

"That's not possible," said Ms. Li. "You'll have to make an appointment and doctor's going away on vacation. Perhaps the first week in October?"

"I've driven a long way," I said diffidently. "I know I should have made an appointment but this matter arose suddenly."

"Are you a lawyer?" Ms. Li asked with dread and distaste. The medical and legal professions view each other as do the mongoose and the cobra, with venomous suspicion.

I handed her my business card.

"Policy is by appointment only," Ms. Li instructed me. Through an open connecting door behind us I could hear the doctor talking on the telephone.

"Please just give him my card and ask him to spare a minute. Policy is never to take no for an answer."

Sure enough, I had found the open sesame. Policy was what it took to move Ms. Li off her great stone wall, policy was more powerful than a thousand threats and a hundred pleas. Obediently, but sourly to register her disapproval, she carried my card into the doctor's office. Some quiet words were exchanged before she reappeared followed by a man of perhaps fifty, in a lime shirt and dark-green checked tie. He had a brush cut and his sandy hair was liberally sprinkled with gray. That was the only liberal thing about him, however; everything else was instinctively nay-saying. You could see it in the high scrunch of his narrow shoulders, and his thin-lipped, pinched mouth. I didn't like him on sight and he had disliked me before he even laid eyes on me.

He looked me up and down. "I'm very busy, Mister"—he rechecked my card—"Henry. Can you tell me what this is in reference to?"

"A nurse who used to work in your unit, Annie Bayard. She's a witness in a case against a client and we're doing a routine investigation of background, character. The usual sort of thing."

As I spoke he was shaking his head no. "I don't recall anyone with that name."

A slim black man in a white nurse's uniform walked into the reception area from the corridor. "Hey, Wu," he said to Ms. Li.

"Have a seat," she answered impatiently, clearly annoyed at the degree to which her domain was spinning out of control. "Doctor has been interrupted."

Hammaker didn't acknowledge the presence of the nurse.

"She worked here until a year or two ago, she told me. She was in charge of a patient named Hanna, Eve Hanna. I believe she left the hospital to go to work for Mrs. Hanna and her husband."

Hammaker kept shaking his head. "Do you recall her, Ms. Li?"

"No," Ms. Li lied. Ms. Li was a bad liar; she tried to make herself look neutral and earnest.

"What did you say was the nature of the legal matter?" Hammaker asked.

"It's a murder case," I said, noticing the involuntary glance that passed between Hammaker and Li. "Someone's life is at stake."

"Lives are at stake every hour of every day around here," he said pompously. "I'm afraid we can't help. I've given you all the help I can and now I'd appreciate it if you would leave. As you can see, I'm very busy."

"Bertie, Bertie, Bertie," I said, "don't be such a jerk."

"Good-bye, Mr. Henry," he said coldly. As soon as he was back at his desk a red light lit up on Ms. Li's phone console. "Yes, doctor?"

"Send in Mr. Traynor now," he said, clearly audible through the open door as well as the intercom.

"Mr. Traynor," Ms. Li said to the nurse, "Doctor is ready for you now."

The nurse had a long plastic face which he arranged now into a look of incredulity, as if Ms. Li's announcement came as news to him. He laid all five of his long, pink fingernails lightly against his chest. "*Moi?*"

"Yes, Mr. Traynor," Ms. Li said crossly.

"Now?"

"Yes, now."

"Oh goody," he said softly, so that Ms. Li and I heard him but Hammaker probably did not. The nurse unbent his flexible, pencil-thin body from his chair. We had to pass close to each other as I started out, and as we did he suddenly bent to tie his shoelace so I stumbled over him, and had to grab hold to keep from falling. As we were disentangling and both going through the, "Sorry, my fault," routine, he whispered against my ear, "Cafeteria." Then he straightened himself and continued into Hammaker's office.

I located the cafeteria, which of course had no windows because it was beneath ground, ordered a cup of coffee and bran muffin, and sat down alone at a table with a copy of the San Jose paper. The Giants had won three straight from the Astros while I had been otherwise engaged in Scottsburg, and had moved within four games of the first-place Dodgers. On the front page, which I looked at after the box scores, league leaders, and transactions, Lost Sam was still burning but containment was now predicted by the next day. The fire had consumed more than one hundred thousand acres.

The most interesting paragraph in the story was the last, as is so often the case. That's where reporters throw in the juicy factlet they couldn't fit anyplace else. It was a quote from

James Myron, the official in charge of the suppression effort.
"The cause of the fire, so far as we have determined, was
lightning that struck near Uncle Sam Mountain. A second
blaze seems to have originated in Lost Valley, fifteen miles
south."

"Mind if I join you?"

I looked up and immediately laid the paper aside. It was
Nurse Traynor. "Be my guest."

He wore not one but two tiny diamond studs in his right
earlobe. There was a can of Sprite and a plastic cup full of ice
cubes in his long, pampered hands.

"Your Dr. Hammaker is a real charmer," I told him.

He popped the Sprite. "But he lacks the essential warmth of
Ms. Li, don't you think?"

"Now that you mention it," I said, smiling.

"It's not his fault, you know," he said, pouring the effer-
vescent soda over the ice cubes. "He's had an anal rod
insertion, standard for heads of service."

This time I laughed out loud. That got me an arched eyebrow from Traynor. "May I see one of your cards?" he asked.
He looked at it briefly before slipping it into the breast pocket
of his white uniform. His name tag identified him as Bruce
Traynor, R.N., Oncology.

"You knew Annie?" I asked.

"Annie was good people."

"I've met her," I said noncommitally.

"You scared 'em pret-ty bad upstairs," he laughed. "Her
name's like a code blue around here."

"Tell me," I said, knowing he would; spilling secrets is a
national pastime.

"Did you ever hear of succinylcholine?" he asked.

"No."

"It's a very potent, rapidly acting neuromuscular blocking
compound. Paralyzes all voluntary muscles, including the re-
spiratory muscles. The patient quietly stops breathing. All
you'd need would be five milliliters, administered IV"

"Try it in layman's terms, would you?"

"Euthanasia. Succinylcholine causes a death that's consistent with serious illness. It metabolizes very rapidly to normal body chemicals, succinate and choline."

"Annie killed a patient?"

"Whoa, whoa, I didn't say that, and if you say I did I'll deny it. The way you survive oncology ward is you shut down your feelings and you do one thing at a time as best as you can do it. Annie, she identified, which is a no-no. She asked for a transfer a few times but they're so understaffed nobody really paid attention to *her* distress signals. So a couple of her patients died, a little girl with leukemia was the first one, and then some old folks. Nobody was killed, you understand? Maybe some processes were accelerated, maybe not. There were whisperings, and even that's strictly *entre nous.*"

"Okay, Bruce, I'll respect the confidence. If I were Hammaker," I said, "or Hammaker's boss, I probably wouldn't want to go into it very deeply if one of my nurses was maybe putting patients out of their pain."

The nurse rearranged his mobile face into a pretty good likeness of Hammaker. "I don't recall anyone called Bayard," he said, sounding just like the head of oncology.

"How hard is it to get your hands on this succinylchlorine, Bruce?"

"Choline," he corrected. He reached into the same pocket where my card had gone. His long longers were closed into a fist when they came out of the pocket. He stretched the fist across the table and slowly opened it. There was an ampule in his pink palm.

" 'Bout that hard," he said. "If you have reason to be in the drug supply cabinet on surgery."

"That's—?"

"I didn't exactly say that, did I?" Nurse Traynor said, smiling as he slipped the ampule back into his pocket. "After Annie left they instituted tighter inventory control. That was, I don't know, year before last maybe. You know how that goes, took tops three months before folks got back to doing things the way they always had."

He took a long swallow of his Sprite and began to suck on some ice cubes. "What's this all about?" he mumbled around the ice. "Our Annie still an angel of mercy?"

I thought of the late Rich Hanna beating up Paul. Of his trying to cheat Peyton out of his land. Of his deserting Annie in her time of need. I thought of the ax embedded in his head.

"It wouldn't surprise me a goddamn bit, Bruce, to tell you the truth."

Eighteen

"You are planning to go to the police about this, aren't you?" Estelle asked, when I finished telling her and Paul about my conversation with Bruce Traynor. We were around the table.

"What can he tell them?" Paul said. "That some nurse up in San Jose who says he'll deny ever saying it thinks that Annie may or may not have put some suffering people out of their pain? They'll just laugh. The cops don't deal in rumors and innuendoes, they need facts to go on."

"Only on television," I said. "In real life most of what they know is just rumor. If it weren't for ill-founded suspicion the police might as well shut up shop. Anyway, you're both right. I will tell Etter at least some of it, and he'll probably laugh at me and say, 'So what?' The fact of the matter is that the sheriff probably doesn't know beans about solving murders except for the kind where two drunks get in a bar fight and thirty-five people are watching when one of them shoots the other."

"Even if Annie did practice euthanasia," Paul said, "does that mean she's capable of killing a man out of anger?"

"Not necessarily, no, of course not. But it does show that

her emotions are strong and deep, and that she's able to disregard the law when she's deeply moved. And," I added, "rage at a man who deserted her and didn't acknowledge his own child is a stronger motivation than pity."

"What now?" Paul asked.

"Well, there's some things I want to check out up in San Francisco, we don't want to put all our eggs in the Annie basket just yet. If Rich was dealing dope the way Peyton said, it's entirely possible that could have something to do with why he was killed."

"But you are going to tell Etter about Annie?" Paul asked.

"Probably, but we're pretty much on our own here."

"Not us, *you*," Paul said. "I feel totally useless."

"Paulie, this is what I do. There's no reason why you should be able to conduct a criminal investigation."

"I know," he said, staring at the table. "Still."

There was a scrunch of tires coming to a stop on the far side of the house.

"I love the way people just drop in," said Estelle. "It's so friendly."

"Maybe you should move out here, Estelle," I told her. "Paul won't admit how much he'd like it if you were here to look after him."

Estelle laughed with delight, though whether at the prospect or the teasing I wasn't sure.

Though the sliding door was open, as always, Sheriff Etter knocked. We all looked up. Paul's face fell, just collapsed instantly with fright and despair. Estelle, sensing that this was her son's enemy, began to scowl belligerently. I went on full alert.

"Sorry to disturb you folks," Etter said. He was a widely built man wearing an ordinary blue business suit. "Mr. Richards, I wonder if we could speak for a bit?"

"Why?" Paul said.

"Well," Etter answered, looking significantly at Estelle.

Paul looked at me for guidance.

"Why don't you tell us what you want to talk about," I said. "And then we'll decide if Paul wants to talk about it too."

"Mr. Richards, this might be better if it was just you and me. Of course, your friend here can listen in if you want, but this is something we can maybe work out together private-like."

"You're kidding, aren't you, Etter?" I said. "You damn well know I'm not just Paul's friend, I'm the defense investigator. And you have no right to talk to our client without his attorney present."

"Well, it's up to you folks then. May I come inside?"

Paul shrugged.

Etter took his hat off and laid it carefully on the table before he took an unoccupied chair. He smoothed down his straight gray hair, then rested his elbows on the table and clasped his hands. They were meaty hands.

"Looks like they'll have this fire pretty much contained by tonight," he said conversationally.

None of us responded.

"Okay. Mr. Richards, we don't get a whole lot of homicides in these parts, I'm sure you know that. We like to clear 'em up, if you know what I mean. I was thinking that maybe we could do each other a turn here."

"Hold it!" I said sharply. "What the hell are you trying to pull here?"

"Hear what I have to say before you jump down my throat, this ain't San Francisco and things work a little differently."

"It is still the United States, Sheriff," Estelle said, "and people still have their rights." Her eyes were bulging angrily and her considerable bosom was heaving. I laid a hand on her shoulder.

"And who would you be, m'am?"

"I am Paul's mother."

"I see, I see." Etter turned to Paul. "Mr. Richards, why'd you buy the ax that was used to kill Richard Hanna the day after he beat you up in the Running Iron bar?"

Estelle gasped. Paul looked bewildered. I spoke quickly, "Don't say a word, Paulie, not a word. That's it," I told Etter. "I think you'd better leave, this is not something we're going to discuss with you."

"Sooner or later you will, if not here then in court. Okay, don't say nothing, that's your privilege. But I'd like you to listen to the rest of what I came to say. We'd as soon not go to all the trouble and expense of a big criminal trial. I bet your smart city lawyer is costing a couple of shekels, too.

"I don't have any trouble understanding a man acting like a man when he's been left no choice. What I'm thinking, all this can be settled without making one of our district attorneys go to court after a first-degree murder conviction. I'm gonna leave now but after I go I think you should have a good talk with your folks here, and with your lawyer, and see if there isn't an easier way for everybody. What I'm telling you is that you've been informed of your rights, including the right not to incriminate yourself, and they're still in effect. If you *want* to talk to me, I'll listen. And if what you got to tell us makes sense, the way I think it will, then we'll be as understanding and reasonable as we can be. That's it."

He stood, turning his hat slowly by the brim with his hands. "We're a small department and we're stretched pretty thin, we got this arson investigation and all, and I jus' think it would be easier all 'round if we find a way to cooperate here."

"I thought it was lightning," I said.

"Up Uncle Sam way, yeah," Etter said. "Usually lightning comes out of the southeast in these parts, but this one circled around and come down the coast. But over in Lost Valley it was a flick of the Bic is what it looks like. We got our ways of finding these things out, you see?"

He put his hat on his head. "M'am," he said, and left.

Paul grasped his temples with both hands. Estelle began to shake and sob. I walked outside and watched Etter drive away. After a few moments, when Paul and Estelle had had a chance to compose themselves a bit, I went back in. Estelle was at the sink, running water into the kettle. She was red-eyed and doing her best to avoid bursting into tears again.

Paul spoke in a wooden, emotionless voice, sounding years older than he was. "There's an explanation for everything but after awhile the explanations don't really matter, do they? That's the real burden of proof." His laugh was brittle and sardonic. "I bought the ax because I was ready to kill that sonofabitch if he came near me again. I wanted to kill him, I wanted to split his skull wide open. I couldn't fall asleep at night for thinking about the humiliation. I wanted to kill him the morning it happened, too, when I saw him starting for my oak. I know how stupid it sounds but I felt a kinship with that goddamn tree, and I took that ax and I went out there to kill that scumbag. Only I couldn't do it. I wish I had, but no, I couldn't.

"How do you think that's going to sound to a jury?" he asked. And laughed again, bitterly.

Nineteen

"Did the DA know about this, or was Etter free-lancing?" Jake Braunstein asked via long distance when I told him about Etter's house call, and his plea bargain offer.

"I don't really know, I've been wondering myself. I guess you'd have to know more about who wears the pants in that family. Should I find out more about it, do you think?"

"Well, yeah, it wouldn't hurt," Jake said. "There's a couple of ways we can go, but my instinct is to start confrontational, seek a restraining order and ask the court to admonish Etter. Send a message that when serious bargaining starts we're not just going to roll over like one of their Saturday night pistoleros with a first-year public defender.

"So, have you talked to the fire fighters who gave statements?"

"Their crew's been shipped out, they're fighting a fire, in Calavaras county, I think. They were both pretty local, weren't they? It won't be hard to go see them."

"Vacaville," he said.

"Inmates or guards?"

"They might as well send the guards to fight the fires and let the cons mind the shop, it may be the Malthusian solution to relieve overcrowding in the prisons."

"Listen, Jake, I'm coming to town for a few days," I said. "Our departed brother Rich Hanna was a grower, he sold some grass up in the city not long before he was mistaken for a yule log. Get in touch with Dink Ebhardt for me, will you Jake, tell him I want the benefit of his expertise. I'll be up tonight, I can see him anytime over the weekend. I thought I'd come out to Tiburon in the morning so you and I can really talk things over, if you want."

"Won't work, Ben, I'm taking Patricia and the kids to Sonoma Mission Inn, there's a mixed doubles tournament she's playing in. Seeded second. Jaysus, look what time it is. I got to get home, we're supposed to be leaving in ten minutes. Listen, here's what. I'll call Dink and tell him you'll be paying a visit this weekend, okay, if he's around. Come around the office Monday first thing, the restraining order'll have to wait. You be sure Paul understands he does not talk to Etter or anybody else without you or me present, yes? So Monday?"

"Sounds fine. Send my love to Patricia, tell her to kick ass."

We hung up.

The upset from Etter's visit still lingered visibly in Estelle and Paul. Estelle was in the kitchen kneading dough for bread, taking it all out on the glutinous lump, banging her pain and anger into sustenance. She wiped her hands on a dish towel slung over her shoulder, then gave me a long, tight hug. I patted her back awkwardly and made clucking, reassuring noises.

Paul's jaw was clenched. He was handling his position the way most straight-john defendants did, thinking about it as little as possible, hoping in this initial stage that it would somehow just work itself out. But Etter's visit had crossed the distance Paul had placed between himself and his fright like a jolt of root canal pain crossing a synapse. He didn't meet my eye.

"You're handling it as well as it can be handled," I said to him. "Only career criminals and lawyers thrive on this stuff, the rest of us just feel like there's a steamroller bearing down on us. Etter'll stay away, Jake's going to get a court order prohibiting him pulling any more stuff like that. It was way off base and I think it was probably intended to scare us because scared people act less judiciously."

"The restraining order," Paul said, "is it something they'll oppose, or is it more or less automatic?"

"Oh, they'll probably say it didn't happen, or that we misinterpreted it. But it has the effect of alerting the judge, and they can't risk it again." I didn't mention anything about building a record for an appeal because I thought it would only worry him more. "He won't chance it, but if Etter shows up again, or anybody else from his office or the DA or anywhere, you say not one word except your lawyer told you to remain silent. But they won't."

Paul laughed again in that brittle, bitter way that was new to him. The bitterness was what I was most concerned about: the fear would pass with the threat, but the bitterness could stain the character.

Estelle had walked over to Paul, and she took his hand. "Our family will come through fine," she said.

Paul did his best to smile at her and pat her hand.

I ducked out at that point. There was a stop I wanted to make before I left for the city even though I knew I might be acting too hastily. Since Jessica Gage had returned home to England to look after her stricken husband I had kept myself to myself, as the English say. I had hurt like hell, then slowly scarred over. Maybe I had been wearing the scar like a badge, letting its emotional authority keep me from other women. So I felt like an excited boy about to ask for his first date as I headed uphill toward Glenn's place, my feet rustling the brown pine needles on the path. I had to watch my step because the thick old root systems were slippery.

It was early Friday evening and the lights were on in the kitchen of the big house, bright and warm in the gloom of the murky forest. Through the window I saw a woman, probably Glenn's wife Sue whom I hadn't met, her head bent and her shoulders moving as she performed some task, but whatever she was doing wasn't visible. The domesticity of the scene, intensified by the brightness of the kitchen light in the woods, exercised a power over my soul: I yearned for what I saw, at the same time I remembered the frustration and boredom of my marriage to Lottie.

Perhaps one hundred feet before it reached the big house the path divided, and I followed the left fork away from the house and toward a smaller structure, not much more than a gazebo. Both sides that faced the path were built of small panes of glass from a point about six feet above the foundation to the roof. The windows were covered with bamboo curtains, and there was a lamp on inside the glass house, as Lil had called her home. A stable door in front was open on top. I stopped a few feet short. Walking all the way up to the open door seemed too startling and intrusive.

"Hello, Lil?" I said.

"Hi." She appeared at the door holding a book in her hand with the thumb marking her place. She didn't seem especially surprised by my showing up. "What's up?"

"I'm driving up to the city for the weekend. You want to come along?" I blurted it out as fast as I could.

With barely any hesitation she said, "Sounds good," and gave me a radiant smile that made me want to jump in the air like some jerk in a Toyota ad. "Give me a sec to throw some things together and I'll be right with you."

I didn't move. She had begun to turn away but when I said, "Hey," very quietly, she turned back inquisitively, her long neck taut and her curls lit from behind by lamplight and streaked with shadow.

I just grinned maniacally at how gorgeous she looked but didn't speak.

"Hey yourself," she said, and was gone.

I went down and waited in the car and it took her no longer than the second she had promised before she was opening the passenger door, throwing a woven wool satchel and an oversize leather shoulder bag into the backseat, and hopping in beside me. She was full of girlish haste.

"I haven't been up to San Francisco, to Berkeley really, since Christmas. I'm excited," she said.

"I am too, but not about San Francisco."

"This is just the ante," Lil said. "Wait until the betting gets serious. Are you going to fold your hand? I think you might."

"You do?" I was crestfallen.

She nodded. "You're trying to find something out but I don't know what you want to know, I can feel it. You feel like a man putting a toe in a bath to see if it's too hot." She lowered a slim, warm hand onto my leg, just above the knee, and rubbed the inside of my thigh slowly back and forth. My throat went dry and I went hard with desire.

Glenn's red-and-white VW van rolled into the path and squealed to a stop in front of us.

"Say, you guys," he hallooed, and started over to us.

Lil moved her hand away and touched her mouth with two knuckles.

"Where you off to?" Glenn asked, leaning against my open window.

"Taking a drive," I said, croaking and clearing my throat.

Speaking across me he told Lil, "Brad's coming 'round, I saw him over Murphy's picking up a load of four-by-tens. He said to tell you."

"Say hi," she said. "Tell him I'll call him. You know that guy Blake something with the CDF? He wants to see you, he had a talk with Sue. It's something about working with a cleanup crew, leading it. He told Sue, she knows about it."

He nodded like wouldn't-you-know-it. "Well, that's nice now that the damage is all done and finished with. Shoot, we should of been the Indian scouts all along, us local men are the ones that know these woods best. I was up to Indian Camp today, and then down over into Spiller Fork, you know, down in that way," he said to Lil, who nodded.

"What's it like in Indian Camp?" she asked.

"These people," Glenn said. "I can't figure out what in hell they were thinking about. That heavy equipment tore out huge old bolls and just buried them under. Those trees were magnificent." His jaw was trembling with anger. "Unspeakable," he said, "what they did to those trees is unspeakable." Then he shook his head angrily, as if to clear it. "Whyn't you both come on up the house and eat with us later on? Sue's making a celebration stew and some folks are coming around. I talked with the bank today and told 'em the overdue payment's comin' just as soon as the CDF pays me what they owe me. They said okay, so that's one less thing."

It wasn't the first time I had seen Glenn make the quick switch from ecological anger to personal affability, and I had begun to see why he and Paul had become friends. Glenn lived close to the surface and by his wits, his life was a juggling act and it gave him a direct and disarming charm. He was concrete, his life was direct and immediate, abstractions didn't seem to weight him down like so many briefcases and traffic jams.

"We're going to San Francisco," Lil said. "Thanks, but we won't be back for supper."

He smiled briefly at this news and glanced now at her bag and mine in the backseat. "Hey buddy," he told me, "be extra careful of those cattle guards, there's two right down by the Hanna place, second one's just past where the road bends around their trailer, first one's between a fifth and a sixth of a mile before that. The way this car's slung low on its axles they'll rip you a new southern exposure if you hit 'em too fast."

"Thanks," I said. "I will."

He rapped twice on the side of the car by way of good-bye, and straightened up.

"Shalom, amigo," I said, and we were off. The moment Glenn was left behind and we were alone Lil and I exchanged ear-splitting grins. She slid over on her seat and snuggled briefly against my shoulder. Her curls felt spongy and silky, and she smelled of soap and a light perfume. Then she sat up yoga-fashion on the wide seat, with her legs crossed under her. Her square shoulders and her hips made a plumb line, and her long back arched beneath a white, sleeveless blouse. The shape of her high, small breasts was soft beneath the thin cotton blouse and some sort of chamois she had on beneath it. She didn't look at me as I watched her. The trees grew right up to both sides of the narrow, sinuous road, and lime-colored Spanish moss drooped from the branches. The houses were widely spaced, and one home was especially beautiful; it was white clapboard, squarish, with a small front porch and green window trim. A western Victorian farmhouse.

Once we reached the state road the smoke in the air thinned out considerably and I saw that the sun was still in the sky, sinking toward the hills to our west. We climbed steadily in silence, both of us engrossed in this sudden opening up of the world after the dark, dungeonlike feel of the forest and the fire. There was a kind of rapture to merely seeing the sun in a blue sky. I pulled off into a view area with a vista south and west over a great distance, and stopped. Ridge after ridge of dark green hillsides—their western slopes, invisible to us, were still in sunshine—rolled away toward the high, jagged peaks of the coastal range. Between the closest ridge and the barely visible coastal peaks was a blanket of white-gray smoke running north and south over a huge area. Here and there isolated fires were burning, sending orange and yellow daggers of flame above the blanket of smoke. From our commanding station you got a sense of the oceanic ceaselessness of the forest. I knew that men had laid many a dirty finger on the river, the hillsides, the trees, but the wilderness remained a place of such purity and pride it made me catch my breath.

"God," Lil said, "it's so sad I could cry."

She walked to the edge of the asphalt, standing her hands in her pockets, stubbing the ground with her toe.

"You know," I said, "when I look at this I feel kind of helpless. I mean I suppose my nature is sort of cynical and suspicious, and I wonder if I don't bucolicize the Hannas and Glenn and Peyton and all you people. You all make me feel that somehow I'm missing the point of life."

"Well, people are just people," she said quietly. "I mean people are troubled everywhere, and have their secrets and their disappointments. The wounding doesn't stop at the city limits, but it's true, living out here gives you perspective. It makes you humble the way city people can't ever be."

"If you're humble in the city you're a victim," I said.

"If you're not humble out here you're not fully alive," Lil said.

After awhile we walked back to the car. "How far are we from the ocean?" I asked.

"Fifteen miles or maybe a bit more," she said. "Why?"

"I don't know, I thought maybe we could get there for the sunset," I told her.

"What is it about men and sunsets? Why do you all want to drive to the beach?"

I laughed. "I don't know," I said. "The truth is that sunsets bore me to tears." All of a sudden I felt free and happy and loose; loose of the fire, of Paul and his troubles, of Estelle's worry, of Etter and the whole business.

We started driving again.

"When I came here to California," Lil said, "it was the winter of nineteen seventy-four; my friend took me out to the beach." She turned, swiveling at the waist, and reached into the backseat, rummaging for something in her wool satchel. She pulled out a pouch of tobacco and her small gold lighter. "To see the sunset, you know? I wasn't really up for it, what I remember best was the graffiti somebody had sprayed on the seawall: NIXON'S DAD SHOULD HAVE PULLED OUT EARLY. I thought, yeah, all right, this is a lot better than Canton, Ohio, for sure."

She opened the Bugle pouch and pulled out an already rolled cigarette. She lit it with the flame from the lighter and took a deep drag. I smelled the acrid sweetness of marijuana.

Lil held the smoke down in her lungs for a moment, then exhaled deeply.

"In Scottsburg we call this stuff the poor person's satellite dish," she said, offering the joint to me.

"Maybe later," I said. It had been a long while since I had last smoked dope.

Lil pulled another lungful down toward her diaphragm. I worked the tin of cigars out of my jacket pocket and began to peel the cellophane off a Dunhill Chico with one hand, keeping the other on the wheel as we negotiated a series of sharp curves. Almost immediately the gold pull tab snapped, and I began to fumble with the cellophane, trying to tear it away without also tearing the cigar apart.

"I'll do it," she said, and took the cigar out of my fingers. She ripped the cellophane with her thumbnail, and the wrapper fell loose. With her thumb and forefinger she undid the ring. She held the cigar in three long fingers, and with her other hand reached into the pocket of my jacket where the cigars had been. She felt around for the clipper, then clipped the cigar expertly, leaving a clean, shallow v-shaped incision in the top.

I remembered her telling me her father had smoked cigars.

She licked the cigar up and down one side and then the other, wetting it before she lit it so it would burn less rapidly. And because it would make me burn more rapidly, which it did indeedy do. Then she put it between her lips and lit it, turning it slowly to make sure it was burning evenly before she handed it back to me.

I drew on it.

"You know," I said, "I don't think I've ever been more grateful to a girl's father in my whole life."

She smiled quietly. "You fly fish?" she asked.

"Some," I answered laconically. An accurate enough portrayal of the two times I had watched a buddy practice at the fly-casting pool in Golden Gate Park.

"No, really," she said, laughing. The best women always see right through you, it's what sets them apart.

"Wait," I said, "isn't the sincere desire to learn a thing fifty percent of accomplishing it? I mean the balance is merely repetition. So the fact that I would like to fly fish amounts practically to having fly fished, right?"

She pulled open the ashtray and laid the joint down in it. "No," she said. She lifted both hands to her hair and pushed it off her neck. There was a fine golden down on the nape of her neck. "The air feels so good," she said.

Both our windows were open and the breeze blew the unlit joint out of the ashtray and onto the carpet. She leaned down and put it away back in the pouch.

"Where'd you get the dope?" I asked.

"Glenn," she said, with her eyes closed. "It's his." That seemed discordant, somehow. We were nearing Monterey. The area was densely populated, with shopping malls and supermarkets, houses and schools built up along both sides of the road. We were back in civilization, no longer in wilderness or in a hamlet but in a countrified suburb, and creeping along in traffic.

Lil reached over and rested a hand lightly on my right shoulder and began to play with the back of my hair, tugging it gently.

"You ever see *Annie Hall?*" she asked.

"Uh huh," I said.

"Remember where he tells her, let's kiss before we eat and get it over with, otherwise my stomach's going to be too jumpy to eat anyhow?"

"Yes," I said. I could actually feel the sudden heat she was generating, and I looked across at her. Her cheeks were a deep pink and her lips seemed swollen. She took off her glasses and smiled conspiratorially.

"You see that motel down there, the Monterey Beach?" She was even speaking differently, slower and throatier. I wondered if I would ever swallow again.

"Yes?" I said.

"Take this exit, let's check in there. I don't want to wait."

Twenty

"I know what it was that rang the wrong bell for me yesterday," I said, sitting upright in the chair where I had been
lounging. Lil and I were finishing a late breakfast in a cafe
south of the Berkeley campus. "You told me that the dope
you smoked last night was Glenn's, and something about that
struck me as being peculiar but I didn't know what until just
this minute. Glenn said over at the Hanna's a couple of days
ago that he had nothing to do with marijuana. He was pretty
adamant about it."

"And?" Lil asked.

"He lied."

"Why, I can hardly believe it," she said, batting her eyes.

"You mean because it's illegal?"

"Glenn was being less than open and honest with you,
investigator. It's his own way of just saying no." She half-
yawned and stretched her arms high over her head, then un-
dulated her square, brown shoulders. I watched her muscles
flex and elongate. She wore a fresh cotton blouse, this one
sleeveless with a scoop neck. The morning sun where we sat
at a white, wrought-iron table on a red brick patio made her

skin appear to be the color of almonds. Golden down shone on her forearms and along her neck.

"I want to ask you a question," she said. "Okay?"

"Shoot," I said happily.

"You think Joe Montana shouldn't have sex the night before a game?"

"I think it depends on who with," I said. "And under what circumstances."

"Wife?" Her feet, in leather sandals, were spread in front of her, and her skirt, a floral print, was drawn up just above her knees.

"Are they getting along?"

"Meaning?"

"Well, if the sex is full of hostility the way it can be, maybe yes, maybe no. But if it's sex without feeling, the kind that leaves a feeling like a hangover, and sticks to your skin and makes you sweat the next day, that's not a good state to carry into a game."

One of her long legs wrapped itself around the back of my knee and squeezed me slowly but strongly until I was caught in the grasp of its silky grip. My testosterone level zoomed right off the chart.

She leaned close to me. "You have a wife or anything?" she said, looking me right in the eye.

I exhaled loudly. "No, no wife." She squeezed me tighter still. I blushed.

"There's someone I've become very attached to. Her name is Jessica, Jessica Gage. She's living in England at present." Having to say it out loud pained me.

"I know," Lil said. "I sensed her absence more than her presence. It comes to pretty much the same really. Are you going to tell her about me?"

"No, I don't think so. There's no reason to." I thought about how to explain. "She's married, we met over here but she's English and her husband was back there. She stayed here with me, but awhile ago he became ill. He had a stroke, a severe one. Jessica wanted to be with him. They are, she says, very good friends. I don't know what the future holds. That's all."

"You love her?"

"Yes," I said. "I do."

Lil was thoughtful, and very still. I could barely tell she was breathing. Her eyes remained open, fixed on the middle distance. "I can live with that, for now," she said. Then slowly, she began to smile at me, conspiratorily, sweetly.

"You feel I threw myself at you?"

"Yeah. Thank goodness," I said, greatly relieved to have it off my chest and so easily handled by Lil.

"What do you want?"

"At this very moment?"

She laughed and squeezed my thumb. "At the moment is an open book and we'll get to that as soon as we can."

Now I laughed. "Beyond the moment?"

"Yep."

"Seriously?"

"Yes."

I knew she was talking about something else, but I gave her the only true answer at the moment. "To find whoever killed Rich Hanna."

"You and Paul are very good friends, aren't you?" She began to slowly shred a napkin into strips.

"We are," I said.

"It's nice the way you don't posture with each other, that's rare to see with men. There *is* something I want to ask you, I'm sorry. But do you think it may be that Paul did kill Rich?"

"I've asked myself, too, a few times I've wondered. Paul told me he didn't, that he wanted to, but didn't. I believe him. Partly, professionally you might say, because I don't have any concrete reason not to. And partly because Paul's one of the very few people in this world I take at face value. He's never lied to me that I know of."

Our fingers and palms began the slow and intricate rituals of longing.

"And now?" I asked her.

"You're going over to the city and look for this Dink Ebhardt character?"

"Uh huh."

"Want company?"

My fingers halted in their tracks. "I thought you had some people here in Berkeley you wanted to see?"

"Phil and Nancy, yeah, I lived with them before I went down to Scottsburg. Listen, investigator, I've changed my mind, okay? There's a lot you don't know about me, naturally, but the first thing you should understand is that I'm alone, I'm on my own. I live in the glass house by myself because that's how I want it." Her expression was reserved and dignified. "Looking for a murderer with you is more exciting than catching up on old times with Phil and Nancy."

"Ah," I said. I didn't know what to say next. I was tongue-tied and bursting with pride and lust on a glorious sun-drenched morning. A sparrow chirped in the branches of a potted Japanese maple. "Okay. Well, let's shove off then."

Lil threw me a snappy salute. "Affirmative. You like being a sex object, huh?"

Twenty-One

"You have reached 555-6144," said the voice on the tape. The voice sounded a great deal like a human being of the male variety but probably wasn't. "If you'd like to leave a message, press one now. Your call will be automatically timed and dated, but please include your phone number with your message. If you're sending a fax, press two now. If you want to speak to someone"—the tape was interrupted by a short, steady tone, and then Dink was on the line himself.

"Dr. Henry, I presume?"

"That's a nifty trick, old man," I acknowledged. Dink was the kind of man whom one could call 'old man' comfortably; irony was lost on him when he was in the throes of techno-pride.

"Simple, really, Stone Age stuff. The answering machine is linked to a computer programmed to display calls from select numbers, along with the name of the phone holder. It allows you to know, for example, if a caller is dialing from any number in the Hall of Justice, even if he is purportedly a good friend of a good friend from Phoenix.

"Our mutual friend said you wanted to powwow with Dink."

"This is true." My syntax around Dink always became confused.

"Come at, just a minute I'm scanning, come at eight-fifteen. Be on time. I can't emphasize this enough—don't park on my block, park at least a full block away. And try not to look so much like a cop."

I let that last remark pass. "There's someone with me." Characterizing Dink as cautious was akin to calling Billy Graham pious. Surprises tended to put him off his conversation.

"By any chance," Dink said, "do you have his date of birth and social security number?"

"Just a minute." To Lil I said, "What's your birth date?" She was slowly swiveling back and forth in my desk chair while I walked around my place with the phone in my hand. Like me, she was wearing only a bath towel knotted around her waist.

"April first, nineteen fifty-nine," she said.

"Know your social security number off hand?"

"For real?"

I covered the receiver with my hand. "The investigations game isn't all fun and fucks, you know."

She told me the number with a wanna-bet smile, and I repeated it to Dink. "You'll hear from me if there's a problem," he said. "Otherwise eight-fifteen."

"Eight-fifteen," I said. He hung up.

"What was that all about?" Lil asked.

I lit us cigarettes.

"Dink runs a unique operation," I said. "He's a wholesaler with a retail outlet. Ever been in a hashish stall in a bazaar someplace like Afghanistan? Dink's market is a Western version, different quality wares set out with little descriptive tags like fancy wines. You're given a time to show up and if you're late you're canceled out, you won't be let in until you make a new appointment. Every twenty minutes another customer

128

comes, that way each one is assured of privacy and the time to make a careful selection. I referred you, which is the first step in gaining admittance; if all you wanted was to buy some dope that would usually be enough. But since I'm asking Dink for information, he wanted to compile a quick dossier on you. Access to Dink's information requires a higher degree of clearance, because information is more dangerous than dope and the penalties for trafficking in it can be summary."

"What kind of dossier?" Lil asked. She ran her thumbs slowly down the can of Classic Coke she was drinking. "What can he find out about me?"

Dink's place was a Victorian on a residential street in the upper Haight Ashbury, close enough to Haight Street to ensure some pedestrian traffic day and night. Farther up the hill, where the views were even better and not beyond Dink's budget, his stream of customers would have been more conspicuous. The house was painted to fit in nicely, but not gussied up with one of those only-in-San Francisco restorations that turns heads. It was peach with gray trim, no less tasteful or more attention grabbing than a Brooks Brothers suit.

At eight-fifteen on the dot Lil and I climbed the long row of steps from the street and rang the doorbell, which played a few notes of "Hey Jude." The camera was discreetly placed so it was invisible from the street. The door lock was sprung electronically, and we walked into a vestibule and began to climb a flight of interior stairs. The steps were carpeted in burgundy and lit by a Tiffany-style chandelier. Dink was waiting for us in the hallway beneath the chandelier.

He was a man of medium height, compact, dressed in an open-neck shirt and pants that were pleated and pressed. He had on argyle socks beneath leather hand-crafted thongs. His handlebar moustache was waxed, and his long, clean-shaven jaw had a bluish cast. There were deep, crescent-shaped lines etched into his cheeks that gave him a look of suffering, an appearance contradicted by the radiant Californian glow of good health, good food, and pots of money. The hand he extended had a gold Patek Phillipe around its wrist.

After we shook hands, he turned to Lil. "Lily," he said, "I'm glad you could come. I had a friend who went to Bowling Green about the time you were there, Carol Ketchum? Did you know her, she was a Tri-Delt?"

"Carol?" Lil said coolly. "Absolutely, we took some courses together and played on the same intramural volleyball team. You guys are friends, huh? What's she up to these days?"

"She's in marketing, in Seattle," Dink said. "Earned a tad under six figures last year. Got a lovely home with an eight-and-a-half percent mortgage and a little ski chalet in Idaho she picked up for a song."

"That so?" Lil said. "She still have that cute patch of freckles on her ass? It was a really weird thing, because, you know, she didn't have freckles anywhere else except on her nose when she was real sunburned."

Dink laughed hoarsely, and nodded his head enthusiastically. "That's what she said, she said you were a big, smart girl with an answer to everything. She did." He looked Lil over, still smiling and nodding. She had on low heels in which she stood not much under six feet, a light skirt and sweater that were not tight but which clung to the clingable parts of her, and a dash of pale lipstick that emphasized the sensuality of her mouth.

"All right," Dink said with approval. "Let's go where we can talk, children." He turned and began to lead us along the carpeted hallway, where little plaster cherubs holding sconces in the shape of torches lit our way past a succession of closed doors. Dink's graying hair was pulled back into a ponytail.

The back room was his office. One corner was occupied by a sleek L-shaped work station, the centerpiece of which was a Compaq 386. There was also a police scanner, a multifunctional telephone console, a fax, a bank of security monitors, a television tuned to CNN but muted, a VCR, and a short-wave radio. There was a modem, plus a lot of unfamiliar computer stuff. Across the room was a wine-colored leather love seat with matching chair and ottoman. Lil and I took the love seat, which creaked with a wonderful leathery sound as we adjusted ourselves. The rug was Persian.

On the wall facing us was a photograph of Janis Joplin, the same photo that had been made into a poster. She looked inexpressibly sad, and was wearing oodles of beads, and was bare breasted. It was signed and inscribed, "I love you, Dink."

"Would you like a glass of wine?" he asked. "I've got an Opus One, an eighty-four, that's ready to be drunk."

"Sure," Lil said. "Sounds good."

Dink went to an antique oak sideboard with leaded glass doors and selected a bottle from a rack. He took his keys out of his pocket and removed the foil with a cutter attached to his keyring. As he began to work the tines of a corkscrew down both sides of the cork, he said, "What are you driving these days?"

"A Seville," I told him.

"Need a cellular?"

"You're dealing in phones that fall off trucks?" I was surprised that he would risk involving himself with pushcart goods.

"There," he said, as the cork came free. "We'll give it a minute or two to breathe." He sniffed the cork and snuck a look as Lil crossed her legs. When he saw me watching him he smiled broadly, showing long white teeth beneath the moustache, and nodded approvingly man to man.

"No, no, nothing like that." He went to a nineteenth-century lawyer's desk, one of those two-sided jobs with a leather inlaid writing surface, where about a dozen plain brown boxes were neatly stacked. He picked one up and slid out a cellular phone.

"Every one of these," he said, bringing it over to show us, "has a memory chip containing a mobile identification number, the MIN. And a second chip with an ESN, an electronic serial number. When you make a call, the ESN and the MIN are automatically transmitted to the carrier, Pacific Bell in our case. Their computer checks the ESN to be sure it's valid. If it is, the cost of the call is billed to the billing number provided by the MIN chip.

"Chips are reprogrammable, of course," he said, smiling knowingly and nodding. "The special feature of these phones is that after your initial investment they're cost-free. Every new technology," he said with reverence, "carries with it opportunities to be bent." Though he had begun his explanation by talking to me about the technology involved, this last boast was directed to Lil.

He put the telephone back on the stack, and brought the wine and three glasses to where we were sitting, handing a glass to each of us, and half-filling them with the dark wine, before he settled into the chair and propped his feet on the ottoman.

"Enjoy," he proposed.

Lil took a sip. "Oh, that's super," she said. "Much, much better than James Arthur Field." I kept a straight face.

"I suppose it is, yes," he said, deflated. Then to me: "Richard Hanna, correct?"

"I suppose Jake told you what there is to tell," I said. "He was murdered, Jake is handling the defendant. Hanna was a small grower, I understand he sold his crop in the city not long before he died, I thought there might be a connection. It presented what we call in the shamus trade," I said, knowing Dink adored words like "shamus," and sure enough it brought a happy grin, "a window of investigative opportunity."

He rolled his wine around in the glass, holding it to the light cast by a brass lamp on the lawyer's desk.

"I never met him myself; we didn't do any business, so what I can tell you is very much secondhand, just so you know. My sources aren't untrustworthy, but my inquiries were, uh, circumspect. Curiosity isn't something people take to positively in my business."

"Okay," I said.

"Not okay, not really. I tell you what I told Jake, I don't like this, I don't like being asked these kinds of questions. Dink Ebhardt is not a fink." He sighed. "Jake holds a lot of my chits, not on paper, nothing to do with money, you understand. You too, same deal. This is something I do as a favor because of what I owe you. I would be happier if you didn't ask me. So. What I hear is Richard Hanna had some problems with his partner."

"Having to do with?"

"Partner trouble always has to do with one thing, doesn't it?"

"Money."

"Uh huh."

"What do you know about the partner?"

"The partner was a silent partner as far as my people know."

"Don't they have a name for the partner? Even a description would help."

"Those are questions Dink can't ask," he said testily. "Those are cop questions." He reached for the bottle and refilled Lil's glass. I shook him off, I only drink wine with food.

"One more thing then," I said. "I'll get you Hanna's birth date and social security number and I'd like a dossier, as complete as possible, with an emphasis on bank transactions. Send it to Jake. And the bill."

"Done," he said. "If you can get me the data on Monday I'll fax my findings to Jake by Tuesday afternoon." To Lil he said, "I don't suppose you require a cellular for your seventy-one Corona, especially since you haven't had even a home phone since you left Berkeley." He stroked his moustache, pleased as all get out with himself.

As we were leaving, Lil asked Dink if she could see the marijuana mart I had told her about.

"I'll see if this is a good time," he said. We were back in the hallway, under the Tiffany, and he went to the closed sliding doors of what had probably once been a dining room, opening and closing them quickly behind himself. When he reappeared, opening the doors, he said, "This will do."

There were two people in the room, a woman sitting on the couch reading *MAUS: A Survivor's Tale,* and a guy, the shopkeeper I suppose, standing at a long picnic table on which the house selections were displayed. From the smell in the air I guessed that the woman was a customer waiting to see how the sample affected her. She looked up and nodded, then went back to reading.

Dink led us along the table. Each quality of grass was heaped loose in hard plastic containers about the size of kitchen drawers, from the least expensive to the most. At the end of the table was a supply of Ziploc bags—a product line that owed its existence to the dope trade—a scale, and some packets of rolling papers.

"Got anything here from down Big Sur way?" Lil asked.

Dink grinned his toothy grin. "Got a question for everything, too," he said. "No, the domestic we're stocking right now is Humboldt blue." He pointed. "Would you care to try some?"

"No," I said quickly. "Thanks."

When she saw my face Lil, who had been on the verge of accepting, said, "No thanks."

"We're expected," I told Dink.

"I understand. Maybe some other time," he told Lil. "Feel free to call. Here's my card." The card contained only his telephone and fax numbers, nothing else.

Lil glanced at it. To Dink she said, "Say hi to Freckles Ketchum next time you get a chance."

Dink showed us out and we walked to the car in silence. Only after we were inside did Lil say, "Why didn't you want me to try that stuff?"

"Dink deals in information. Even your friend's freckles are in her file, you don't want a record of your purchasing dope in there too. He's been busted twice and sooner or later he'll be busted again, and then you'll be in the DEA's computer too. That's all. So, what did you think?"

"Of him? He wanted to get in my pants." She still had his card in her hand. Now she folded it in half and ripped it across the middle.

The gesture was perfect and complete. For a moment I thought of Jessica Gage with regret rather than longing, more like a memory of love than a woman I loved.

"What about Rich's partner?" I asked. "Were you aware that Rich had a partner?"

"That surprised me," she said. "But there's some people I can ask when we get back down there. Glenn might know something, or Minerva, a friend of mine who works sometimes as a mule."

"You were great," I said.

"Was I?" She was pleased.

"You were. You handled him beautifully."

"Handling men isn't very hard," she said. "They only want two things, a good body and to be comforted, in that order."

"And women?" I asked. "What do they want?"

"I want to be excited, to be adored, to be treated gently, with consideration and understanding."

That knocked the wind right out of my jocularity. "It's a tall order," I said soberly.

Lil smiled at me in a new way, as if she believed in me, and all this wasn't entirely fun and games.

"You're a tall guy," she said quietly.

Twenty-Two

"Read that," Jake Braunstein said, handing me a sheath of papers and putting his feet up on his desk, tilting back, and waiting for me to finish. He tossed a furry yellow tennis ball in the air while I read a statement from Vernon Tully, one of the hotshots who had observed the exchange between Paul and Rich Hanna moments before an ax blade had silenced Hanna for all eternity. The statement had been taken by Sheriff Etter and the assistant DA handling the case. Tully had seen Paul run up the hillside carrying an ax and shouting. He had seen him, "swinging that ax around, threatening-like," at Hanna. Since at the time Tully was busy chaining fallen trees to a tractor, and since his vision of what was happening was obscured both by distance and smoke, he had not seen how the ax ended up imbedded in Hanna's head. But it appeared to him that Paul had been, "fried, man, ready to kill that dude on the dozer."

"Inconclusive," I said, when I finished reading.

"Absolutely," Jake said, still tossing.

"And impeachable," I added. "This guy's doing a stretch

for larceny. The two key words here are sure to be parole and date."

"No question about it," Jake said.

"So no problem then."

He put the ball down on his desk and laced his fingers behind his head. He was wearing a blue shirt with a white collar. His initials appeared not only above his heart but on his cuff links, leaving him in no doubt whatsoever as to his identity. Or his clients as to his fee structure. "The problem is Paul running up that hill brandishing the ax in a threatening manner. He doesn't have any duty to retreat from deadly force, right? If Hanna had been threatening the house, or threatening Paul, or anybody who might have been in the house, with deadly force, i.e., the bulldozer, then Paul would have been within his rights to defend himself. If the bulldozer, however, was a considerable distance up the hill, and Paul charged up there waving his ax around as if it were his intention to threaten Hanna, well . . ." he said, "then we need a more applicable theory to fit those facts. Here, here's the other witness statement, from one Gordon P. Coleman. He saw even less than Tully but he saw Paul approaching the bulldozer too."

"Yeah, but Hanna was starting to plow under an oak tree that didn't need to be uprooted."

"Threatening trees isn't punishable by death even in California," Jake said dryly.

"The important thing," I told him, "is that Paul didn't kill the schmuck."

Jake lifted his thick eyebrows, one of his most effective gestures. "You're sitting here in my very comfortable, very costly client's chair telling me with a straight face that my client didn't do it? None of my clients ever did it, none of my clients ever will have done it. Ergo, what the fuck difference does that make?"

"I'm going to find out who killed Rich Hanna," I said with more conviction than I felt. "You keep Paul out of court until I do." I listened to myself and didn't like what I heard. "I'm sorry, Jake, the guy's my oldest friend, his mother helped raise me, and I know what I sound like, I sound involved. But I've developed some good leads." I proceeded to tell him about Annie Bayard's background as an angel of mercy in San Jose, Peyton's property grab, and of the existence of a disputatious partner in Hanna's growing venture.

"I wish you could hear yourself," Jake said when I was finished. "According to you, every hayseed in Scottsburg was nursing a homicidal grudge against Hanna. Leaving aside that except for the property thing none of it is admissible, but even if we do get some of it in, it'll backfire. What does it prove except that Hanna was an eminently killable human being? And how does that help Paul?"

"It helps if I find who did it."

"And furthermore . . . aw jeez, Ben, c'mon. C'mon! All right, I'll humor the man. Amid this nest of vipers, whose sting do you think was deadly?"

"I'm not sure. Annie is angry and defensive, like she's hiding something."

"Uh huh, well, in my experience she's alone among our fellow citizens in that."

"Peyton's shrewd and calculating."

"Should run for DA," Jake said. "Oh, did I mention that Dink faxed us this morning? Giselle's getting him the information on the birth date and whatnot off the coroner's report."

I was dispirited by Jake's detached cynicism, probably because it so resembled my own when I wasn't so involved in a case. "Good," I mumbled.

"Listen, what about the incident with Etter? I'm still inclined to go for a restraining order. I want you to leave a statement with Giselle.

"I don't want to discourage you, buddy-o," Jake continued. "If you find something solid, great. But meanwhile let's start constructing Paul's defense with what we know we've got. Get up to Vacaville and talk with those witnesses," he said, gesturing at the statements. "Round up some character witnesses, you know, I don't have to instruct you."

"Peyton told me Rich Hanna threatened to kill him over the property thing," I said. "That'll fit in nicely with self-defense."

He looked at me appraisingly. "Your chin's gonna wear a hole in my new carpet. Come out to the house tonight, for some goddamn reason Patricia wants to feed you."

"Thank her, Jake, but I'm going back down there today. I just . . . I came in here thinking that things were moving slowly but steadily, you know?"

"You came in here, my friend, sorely in need of an objective correlative," Jake said.

Twenty-Three

"A penny," Lil said.

"Aren't worth that much," I grunted. I kept my eyes on the road rather than respond to her look. We rode on in renewed silence.

Lil went into her bag, came out with a harmonica and began to play, "Me and Bobby McGee," which was wryly appropriate to the journey and the mood I was in. The music made me happy-sad. I slid my hand onto her lap and she crossed her legs, capturing it between. I wondered if the picture of Janis in Dink's place had, like the proverbial grain of sand, grown in Lil into this song of Pearl's.

Though it wasn't the fastest route I followed Highway 1 along the cold blue sea. A thick pillowy fog bank was piled up a few miles offshore. But at land's edge the day was bright and clear as we wended our way past Devil's Slide with its sheer drop to the foam-licked dun beaches, and then inland through pumpkin patches and artichoke and spinach fields on either side of Half Moon Bay. At the huge hydroelectric plant north of Santa Cruz Lil suggested we stop and have lunch on the pier.

"What did that lawyer say to you anyway to turn you into a bear?" We had parked the car near the arcade, and were walking back toward the pier. Lowriders and chopped-off bikes burped and revved along the seaside, fender-to-fender with tourists in their Toyota rentals and family vans. Volleyball games were being contested on the sand by vacationing students whose sleek, brown bodies seemed inexhaustible sources of pleasure and energy.

"That I lacked an objective correlative," I told her. "Besides proving that he took a lit-crit course as an undergraduate, I think he was saying my mind is muddied by how badly I want to get Paul off the hook."

"Is that such an awful thing, caring?"

"Only when it clouds clear judgment."

"Judgment," Lil said dismissively. "Caring takes you deeper into things."

I thought about what she had said in silence. She slung a friendly arm around my shoulder as we started along the old plank pier. A good body and comfort, how right she was.

"Judgment," I said, "is what shows you where to dig deep. Like a coal miner, his lamp is his judgment and his pick is his caring."

She laughed. "Isn't it good," she said, and it wasn't a question. The blue sky, the balmy air, the anticipation of good food, the lithe kids on the sand, were all like stage lighting and painted sets to thrust forward the play: we were the thing. I slipped my arm tightly around her feathery waist.

We ordered fried scallops and clams, and iced teas, and sat at a picnic table in the sunshine, eating with our fingers. Lil had on a green silk Hawaiian shirt and wore a bright red ribbon tied around her hair; the upswept hair highlighted her long, delicate cheekbones. When we were finished eating, she tore her bread into pieces and tossed them to the caterwauling gulls, who snatched them out of the air clean and swift as Willie Mays in his youth.

"You're musical," I said.

"Just shy of professional quality," she answered. "The clarinet's my instrument, the harmonica's just fun."

"And you danced?"

She nodded and tossed the last hunk of sourdough high into the sky. "Better than I played; I studied seriously until I was fifteen."

"And?"

"My mom's ambition was for me to dance with a ballet company. By fourteen I was as tall as I am now, and that was too tall. I quit at sixteen. My dad's genes played her a lousy trick."

"I wanted to be a jockey," I said. "I don't know why, I never was around horses. I was too tall, too, by junior high. I guess we both outgrew our ambitions."

"Before we ever grew into them," she agreed. "You like what you do now? Investigations?"

"It suits me well enough," I said. "I used to be a newspaper reporter and I drove a taxi too, transitionally. I think I just like nosing around in other people's business."

She sucked the dregs of her iced tea through a red-and-white-striped straw. "What are you going to do now?"

"You mean if all these people weren't watching?"

She laughed and rubbed my ankle under the table with her foot. "I mean about Paul, Rich, that whole mess."

The bad feeling was there again. "Dammit," I swore, and whacked the picnic table. I sighed. "I don't know, confront Annie Bayard maybe, tell her what I found out and see if the surprise makes her stupid or desperate. I want to know more about what actually happened between Peyton and Rich, Dink's stuff might shed some light on that."

"Peyton didn't kill Rich," Lil said.

"He didn't? How can you be sure?"

"He's too weak, I don't mean physically weak. It took someone strong to do that."

"Annie then?"

"Possibly," Lil said.

"But you aren't really convinced?"

"She could have, I don't know, but I have an instinct she didn't."

"I suppose what's getting to me is that I'm at a point where all I can really do is wait and watch until something I see or hear or think sets me moving again. Waiting is not exactly my strength."

"What did the lawyer think? Did he have any good ideas about who did it?"

"Just about who didn't do it," I said. "That's how criminal lawyers approach things. First cops figure out who did something, then lawyers figure out who didn't. His job is to prepare a defense for Paul, and he's good at that."

"Well, Paul needs a good defense," Lil said.

"You do think Paul did it, really, don't you? You don't have to skirt around it."

"I don't know who did it," Lil said, reddening. "You're putting words in my mouth."

"I—"

"You're frustrated and angry at yourself, investigator, that's what."

A touchy silence lasted until we began to walk back toward the car. I was fishing around in the rusty bait box of my mind for something to lure her closer again, and I came out with, "How long do you figure to stay in Scottsburg?"

"Mmm, hard to say. This year for sure; I'm signed up to drive the school bus again starting in September. After that, who knows? I'd like to see Japan."

"You're able to live on what they pay you for driving the kids to school?"

"Well, you've seen my place," Lil said. "And Sue and Glenn let me stay rent-free."

"That's nice of them."

"It certainly is, but they've been able to afford it okay. Sue's got a good job down at Miracle Construction in Carmel, and Glenn had his little gardening business mostly at homes in CV, and some kind of trust or something."

"What was all that when we were leaving about him being short on the mortgage?"

"Well, the house is his, he had it from his folks before he met Sue; and the drought's cut way into his income, you know, people aren't doing anything with their gardens like they did in other years. And there's some hitch about his trust, I think. Sue mentioned something, it didn't come through or something this year, so they've been kind of tight."

We had reached the car and could hear the calliope music on the boardwalk, and the happy screams of people on the rides.

"You want to try the roller coaster?" I asked.

"I have a better idea," she said, taking my hand and leading me into the seaside arcade called Cocoanut Grove. Inside it was brutally noisy, and thick with hundreds of kids routing electronic bad guys. Evildoers were dying in a blaze of missile fire as exploding bombs illuminated decaying buildings, army helicopter gunships leveled farmhouses leaving only scorched earth, a killer clown took it in the windpipe, psychos and slavering attack dogs lunged for damsels only to be blown apart with replicas of AK-47s. The mayhem was graphic and personal.

I stood in the middle of the cavernous room, turning slowly through three hundred and sixty degrees of bloodshed consuming the hormonal aggressions of puberty.

"Go ahead, big boy," Lil said, her eyes shining with merriment. "Get in there and kick ass."

Twenty-Four

Lil was leaning in the car window where I had pulled up near the path to her house, giving me a so-long kiss, when Tommy Garber came running toward us, clearly excited.

"Mister . . . Henry," he gasped, winded and choking on his words in his haste to get them out. "Mister . . . I been . . . I done like you said, I seen some stuff in a secret hiding place kind of, it's up Railly Canyon." He pointed.

"Hey, Tommy," Lil said. "How you doing?" She spoke softly and put an arm around his shoulder, giving him a calming squeeze.

"Lil, lissin, like I tole Mr. Henry, this hiding place, secret hiding place, with a compass 'n' a pack 'n' canteen, 'n' there's . . . I was walkin' up that way the mornin' grandma passed on and nobody saw me or anythin', and I saw this tarp, this, in the hollow of a redwood, with leaves and branches over it like nobody was supposed to find it or—"

"Tommy," Lil said sharply, exchanging a significant look with me, "Tommy, did you say your grandma passed on?"

"Yes'm, it's made everybody sad, me too, and grandpa's

not sleeping any 'cause he's over at Uncle Roy and Aunt Ellen and him'n Roy and dad is making grandma a coffin."

Lil's big round eyes shone wetly, and the muscles in her throat worked. "Tommy," she said not much louder than a whisper, "Where's your mom and dad?"

"Dad's up with grampa. Ma's at the trailer with everybody," he said. "Mr. Henry, c'mon up Railly Canyon way, it's *real* suspicious."

Lil squeezed my forearm hard and walked off toward the Hanna clan's trailer. Tommy and I both looked after her, then Tommy looked at me.

I saw in his face that he knew what was happening, it was grown-ups behaving in their usual inexplicable way, with their usual capricious and mixed-up priorities. "I'll show you where," he said, already knowing that his cause was lost. "It won't take but a minute."

He might have lived sixteen years, but emotionally he couldn't have been more than ten. He seemed so vulnerable, this little boy in the loutish, overweight body. It was transparent how easily he could be wounded by anyone to whom he had attached his affections.

On the road behind him I saw Roy Hanna and Roy, Jr., drive by in the little white Toyota pickup, and swing into the long drive to the Hanna encampment five hundred yards along the road, the same direction Lil had gone. Then I returned my full attention to Tommy.

"Up Railly Canyon, huh? It certainly sounds suspicious, no doubt about it. You have any ideas what it was there for, what's behind it?"

He squirmed and looked at me shyly with his head lowered. "Loot?"

I nodded, tight-lipped. "A possibility, a distinct possibility."

He was so pleased, he ran around and opened the passenger side door. "I'll show you," he said, climbing in.

I waited until he was inside so I could put my hand on his knee. "Tom, listen, I'm going to come see what you've found but I've been up in San Francisco doing some investigating of my own, you see? There's a couple of things I've got to check out first. Things," I added portentiously, "I wouldn't want anybody to know about. You understand?"

He nodded, both crestfallen and enraptured.

"Okay, then. I'm going over there first and express my condolences to your grandpa and your mom and dad and all. But I want you to help me out some more, if you're willing?"

"Yes, sir," he said.

"First, I've got to know something. It's okay with your mom and dad if you're up in Railly Canyon on your own, isn't it?"

"Sure," he said, a little disappointed that I didn't know something so patently obvious.

"Good. Now, this clue you found up there, it fits in with some other stuff I've learned in my own investigations. I want you to keep an eye on it, check it out every day, make sure nobody makes off with it. Will you do that for me? And then as soon as the other pieces are in place I'll go up there with you. The way an investigation works, it's like a jigsaw puzzle, you've got to put the pieces together in just the right order. There's a few more pieces I've got to find before I check out this loot angle, okay? A detective's motto has got to be a time for everything and everything in its own time."

He thought about it. "Mr. Henry," he said, "what's condolences?"

I fought down my smile. "It means like if you're sorry at something that happened."

He nodded.

"You going to come up with me?" I asked, getting out of the car.

"Yep," he said.

The earthen lane was littered with brushlike wands of fallen needles from the firs that towered above us. The air still smelled like a cold grate, but the smoke and ash weren't nearly as thick as they had been, and the sun was clearly visible. Long, lazy shafts of light penetrated the gaps in the high

147

branches, and you could see particles of white ash twirling in the radiant columns. I was thinking how much easier it was to play make-believe detective with Tommy than to get a handle on the real life mystery of who had murdered Rich Hanna, and why. And at least there was an answer to that mystery even if I never discovered it. But was there an answer to why a sweet person like Tommy was the way he was? Or the mystery of how my heart was turning toward Lil. I thought to myself that I must write to Jessica and say something. But what? It would keep, it would have to.

Lil was at the long table of victuals with the women. Three little kids were clinging to her. I nodded but went on by to where Roy was standing by the truck. He ignored my approach. His hands were jammed into the back pockets of his Levis, and he was looking toward the hillside, his straw hat pushed back on his head revealing the milky-white top of his forehead.

"Hello, Roy," I said. "I'm sorry about your loss."

He met my eye. His face was both fierce and composed as he nodded thanks. He pulled his hat firmly down into place. "That old lady did all she could," he said huskily. Then he shouted, "Roy, what in hell's keepin' you, boy?"

Young Roy came out from behind the green trailer, carrying a power drill and a box of bits.

"Couldn't find the copper screws," he said to his father. "Somebody moved 'em from where I put 'em."

Old Roy got in behind the wheel of his truck.

"Howdy," Roy Jr., said to me courteously. There was something of both his parents in the appealing manner of the eldest son: the competency and knowledge of his father combined in him with his mother's gentler spirit.

"I just heard about your mom," I said. "I wanted to tell you I was sorry."

He nodded silently, the same gesture precisely as his father's, shifting his leather cap on his skull. "Thanks," he said. "She died real peaceful and pa and us kids were all there, the doc had come by and everything when she took a turn."

Now I nodded, and wondered if my father, whom I could only vaguely remember, had once nodded in just this same way.

"Well," he said, "got to get back." He climbed in, and his father punished the gas pedal before Roy Jr., had even slammed the door.

Twenty-Five

I headed toward Lil, who had one little boy on her lap and two other children pressing close. She was engrossed in the kids, and I in the tableau the four of them presented so the one hard word Annie Bayard threw at me stopped me cold.

"Git!"

Annie was standing a few feet to my right, her short legs spread wide, her hands clenched at her sides, a whip curled into her right fist. Our eyes held. Annie's eyes were filmed over with rage, and I sensed she was going to lash me. I didn't know what I would do if she did strike me, whether the sex of the actor or the act itself would determine my response. The corner of her mouth trembled, and a thin scar I hadn't noticed before shone white against the heated pink of her cheek.

"I'll only say it this once, git!" I looked again into her eyes but there was nothing to see: they were black and opaque, her reason was overwhelmed by the powerful fright I evidently caused her. I had no doubt at that moment that with almost any provocation she was capable of murdering me, or trying to, on the spot.

I nodded, "I'm on my way, I just wanted to tell you I'm sorry about Mrs. Hanna." Calling Eve Mrs. Hanna stung her, as I hoped it would. Then I turned my back on her because I knew it would be harder for her to strike me with the whip if I weren't looking. As I walked away I saw that Tommy Garber had crept from wherever he had been and was now among the children drawn up around Lil.

Nobody moved and not a sound was made as I walked through the clearing around the smoldering ash can. I was a stranger and this was a clan in mourning. Very few people there had any understanding of why Annie feared and loathed me: what they did know was that I had no place among them. As I reached the track at the far end of the sun-dappled clearing and started through the trees, a little girl shrieked, "Freddie, you cut it out!" There was a second, childish yelp of response, and then adult voices, four or five at once, admonished the children, and a curtain of human chatter dropped behind me and closed me out.

At just that moment I stumbled over a fallen pine cone and nearly lost my balance. As I plunged forward, trying to keep myself upright, a jolt of pain shot from my ankle to my brain and back again in the time it took me to catch myself.

"Damn," I muttered. Each step hurt but I was determined not to show that anything was wrong, in case I was still being watched by somebody in the Hanna compound. Inwardly I gritted my teeth and made myself pick up my pace without favoring my aching right ankle.

"It's not possible, is it?" Estelle asked. I had just finished describing what had taken place since I had last seen her and Paul on Friday, with a heavy emphasis on Annie Bayard.

Estelle answered herself: "Do you think the woman's husband knows, if it is true I mean?"

"Yes," Paul said. "She wouldn't have done it without his say so."

"The question is," Lil said, "did Eve know?"

Lil was right, of course.

"You mean," Paul said, "because if this was something Eve wanted, then what we're looking at is not morally unambiguous by any means—if she wanted to die now then really it's a kind of suicide. Isn't it? But if someone else made the decision for her—well, even Roy is one thing. But Annie. I mean, she didn't have the right to make that decision."

"That may be how Rich Hanna saw it too," I said, remembering the force of Annie's blind rage.

Estelle leaped to her feet, she was surprisingly nimble for her size. "My cake," she said, and rushed to the oven.

"Devil's food?" I asked.

"It is still your favorite, isn't it?" The heat rushing from the open oven fogged her glasses, and she took them off and laid them aside. Then she pulled the cake out of the oven with padded pink oven mitts. "Don't let me interrupt what we're talking about," she said, a little too brightly, and dabbed at her eyes with a mitt, lifting the dark cake high.

Paul slid his chair back from the table and walked over to his mother. He took the cake out of her hands and put it down; then he wrapped his arms around her, and she threw herself into him, burying her face in his neck and weeping loudly. Paul rocked gently, comforting her. Estelle's oven mitts were pressed against his shoulder blades.

When she had regained her composure, she said, "I'm just so scared, I'm sorry. I should be ashamed of myself."

"We're all scared, ma," Paul said. He removed one glove and took her hand in both of his. Her age showed in the liver spots on the backs of her hands and the slight swelling in her knuckles. Paul kissed the back of her hand.

Estelle pulled a tissue out of her pocket and blew her nose. "I want to ask you all something," she said. "Is this our business? Isn't this what the police are for?"

"If we go to the police, Estelle," Lil said sympathetically, "and we're wrong about Annie, we would have to be prepared to live with what we'd done to that family. This is a time of need for them."

"And," I added, "to what we'd done to Lil and Paul. Paul would be through here."

"Lil," Paul said, resuming his seat with us at the pine table. "I appreciate your concern, the concern you've shown for me all along. And I value your opinion, but maybe it would be the best thing for you to go on home. You don't have to stay here and be a part of this, I wouldn't want my problems to hurt you in some way."

"That's sweet, Paul, I thank you. But I am a part of this now. If Annie killed Eve, or Rich as far as that's concerned, and I went on home and read my seed catalogs and pretended to forget all about it, then I really would be washed up here. You see?"

Paul nodded solemnly but I could see he was close to smiling also. "I do," he said.

"Listen, we've got to stay mindful of Roy, too," I said. "He's like a wounded animal now, liable to turn on anyone he sees as hurting him or his family. He's losing his home, he's lost his wife, his forest is burned. Whatever is going on with Annie, I pretty much agree with Paul. There's a good chance Roy knows more about it than we do, whether it was his decision or not. I think he could be dangerous if we start blundering around asking questions. What I'm asking myself is, if we don't want to go to the sheriff with our suspicions, and if we can't risk investigating further on our own, where does that leave us?"

There was a longish silence.

"Roy Jr.," Lil said, "if there's anyone at all from over there we could talk to about this it's Roy Jr."

"Roy Jr.," Paul agreed.

"Not a word, not one single word, until that woman is decently buried and her family has had a chance to mourn her," Estelle said. "Do you hear me?" She looked at all of us in turn. "Now if nobody minds I've got some chocolate icing to make. Paul, is there a wood mixing spoon in this house?"

Twenty-Six

Everybody else had gone off to the funeral. It seemed best, considering what had happened the last time I saw Annie, for me to stay away. So I was alone with the devil's food cake on Tuesday afternoon when the telephone rang.

"Mmlo?" I said around a mouthful of spongy chocolate.

"Is Ben Henry there?" asked a woman, officiously.

"I believe so," I said, swallowing. "Who's calling please?" Small lies and distortions are, I believe, a sign of a trustworthy character. Those who never lie are moral eunuchs, untested.

"Mr. Braunstein's office."

"Giselle?"

"Ben?"

"Oh," I gasped, "be still my throbbing heart."

Giselle had raised four sons and knew all about boys. "Oh dear me, have a sip of water. I'll put you on hold until you calm down."

"Giselle!"

"Yes?"

"Anything, but not hold."

"You ask a lot but then we've come to expect that from

you. Dink Ebhardt faxed us several sheets for you. How would you like them delivered?"

I thought about that. "Telephonically," I said.

"All of it?" Giselle sounded unenthusiastic.

"Have you had a chance to glance through it, by any chance?"

"I'm doing that now. It's a financial dossier for Richard David Hanna, born August sixteen, nineteen fifty-three. What do you want to know?"

"Give me an idea of what's in it and I'll stop you when I want more."

"Okay, car is a nineteen eighty-six Chevy pickup, fully paid for. No hospitalizations as far back as Dink went which was nineteen eighty-four, but a visit in nineteen eighty-five to a hospital emergency room for multiple fractures and lacerations following an auto accident. No health insurance.

"Spotty credit bureau report. BofA Visa, Wells Fargo MasterCard. J. C. Penney's. Let me see, the MasterCard's current and the Visa's over its two thousand dollar limit.

"He subscribes to *Playboy, Logger's World*—"

"Did Dink come up with anything on his bank accounts?" Bank transactions and account balances were not available through any of the data bases where Dink had culled this other information, I knew. Banks were close-lipped and required an inside contact willing to breach the rules. This was the junction where Dink's drug interests came together with his information services as easily as some words just naturally combined with others to form powerful adjectival phrases such as free dope or implied threat.

"He's a grower?" Giselle asked.

"Yes," I said, "but how do you know?"

"His current balance is just over sixty-five thousand dollars. His balance at the end of the last two quarters were four thousand dollars in March and three hundred and thirty-five dollars in June. The sixty-five thousand dollars was deposited August fourth. I see this stuff all the time, you know, and it's always the same. These guys are all harvest rich and summer poor. At least this one was sensible enough to pay off his car and his house when he could afford it."

"You're a marvel. How'd he do last year?"

"Not so hot. The August deposit was only for $28,000."

"Well, this wasn't such a great year for him anyway. Somebody murdered him last week, this is the guy Paul Richards is supposed to have done in."

"Anything else you want from us?" Giselle asked.

"Oh," I gasped, "be still my throbbing—"

The next thing I knew, I was listening to a Bach three-part invention, consigned to the contemporary purgatory of being put on hold. I stuffed another bite of cake and thought about Rich Hanna's finances. The sixty-five thousand dollars he scored represented either an expanded crop, or the source of his partner trouble. The latter, I thought: he had stolen his partner's share of this year's profits. The Bach was cutoff in midphrase.

"There," Giselle said sweetly, "did it move for you too?"

Twenty-Seven

After the funeral Paul and Estelle arrived back with Lil, Glenn, and his wife Sue. I hadn't met Sue before. She had a long face with pronounced cheekbones and large, regular features. Sue wanted to come across as a hale-gal-well-met, but it would have been hard to mistake the dissatisfaction in her brown eyes and the resigned set of her mouth. Her hands were red and dry and filigree-webbed, and she wore rings on six fingers. Glenn brought around a gallon of red wine, and the mood and conversation was shrouded by the funeral, so it never seemed appropriate to bring up Rich or the partner he had cheated.

Everybody else drank red wine but I stuck to beer, and about the time the jug was more empty than full, Sue suggested that "the girls" head out on their own into Carmel Valley village, CV she called it. Estelle put up a token protest but was secretly pleased to be invited along. Lil fell in easily with the plan.

Before they left, Lil came over and laid a cool hand on the back of my neck, tugging my hair as she leaned close to kiss my ear. She whispered, "I've got something to tell you."

Glenn, watching us, whooped: "Hey, lookee here!"

"Where have you been?" Sue asked. "Mars?"

Estelle was studiously ignoring this byplay, opening her handbag and examining its contents. "I really shouldn't be doing this," she said for the third time. "You girls would have a better time by yourselves."

Lil whispered, "It will have to wait, okay?"

Sue yelped, "C'mon Estelle, you'll drink us under the table." She and her husband, I noticed, parted without any sign of affection being passed.

The three of them left with that warm, busy bustle that only can be generated by small groups of women heading out a door. We all took sips from our glasses when they were gone, Paul and Glenn and I.

"The ladies, God bless 'em," I proposed. "It would be a brutish life indeed without their touch."

Paul laughed in his nose. He knew a lot of things but not about women. With women he tried too hard and in all the wrong ways. Paul had never understood the real, unspoken language of the sexes: he kept sending demand notices to women awaiting handwritten pleadings.

"I thought it was going to be a lot more of a strain having my mother here," Paul said. "She's behaving herself really well. The truth is, she always does and it always takes me by surprise."

"Estelle's just grateful to feel she's doing something," I suggested.

Paul smiled. "Devil's food cake."

"Your ma baked a devil's food cake?" Glenn said. "Shoot, any left?"

"It's out there in the kitchen," Paul said, waving a touch unsteadily in that direction.

Glenn scraped his chair back, and went for the cake. He cut three slices. The first two he carried to the table on the open palms of his heavy hands and put down in front of Paul and me. The lines in Glenn's hands were ingrained in black.

He took a big bite out of his own wedge of cake and washed

it down with red wine. "I was talking to this guy over at the base camp," he said, "like a captain in the CDF, from around Redding way. He says the arson guys are ninety-five percent sure that sucker was set." He had that knowing grin.

"Yeah, Etter said the same thing," Paul said. "The sonofabitch. What did this guy you talked to know about it?"

"Well, whoever lit it, lit it in that campground up in Lost Valley. You ever been in that way?"

Paul shook his head no. He was nibbling at his cake, breaking off tiny pieces one at a time.

"Me 'n' Sue hiked in there once, God it's beautiful. Like a little canyon. There's this little spring, it makes a pool maybe eight or ten feet in diameter, maybe six or eight feet deep, ferns, flowers. All the mosses and everything. I wonder if it's still there? Suppose not, prob'ly like it got napalmed."

"Were you in Vietnam, Glenn?" I asked.

Glenn raised his brow and the beak of his straw hat bobbed. He scratched his forehead at the hairline. "Spent my war mostly in Napa State, starting when I was nineteen and waitin' to be drafted, this was nineteen sixty-eight, and I was just having myself a big party. Big never-ending round-the-clock devil-may-care electric-Kool-Aid-acid party."

He nodded his head, his bulging eyes glowing with pleasures remembered and not regretted. "Shoot, Paul's heard about this before."

Paul filled his own glass and passed the jug to Glenn. Glenn slung it behind his shoulder and lifted his glass, tipping the bottle over his shoulder and splashing his shirt as he refilled his glass.

"Tell Ben about the bus," Paul said.

"No big deal," Glenn said, "I was trying to get up where this lady lived on Mount Tamalpais, up north of San Fran. I missed the last bus out, partying like always, and this ticket seller, he was like, you know, 'fuck off asshole, the next bus ain't till eight o'clock in the morning.'

"There was all these buses out in the yard there, and I needed to sleep, so I climb on one back in the yard, back near

159

the shop, to curl up and wait for the bus to Tamalpais. Thing that tripped me up, some sucker left the key in the ignition. I really was hot to see this lady, she had the most perfect tits you've ever seen.

"I'd never drove an interstate but I checked out the transmission and all and it didn't seem any too complicated, just a little old Allison D740 automatic four-speed. I sat there a spell waiting to see if anybody's coming to check up and the next thing I know I'm on that bridge, that kind of crooked one that goes on around San Quentin?

"God, I'm tellin' you, that prison looked like the end of the goddamn world, the towers all lit up and the walls so thick and black. I could *feel* the men sleeping inside those cages inside them walls, how their dreams were like snakes all twined and looped around each other. More snakes 'n' anybody'd ever seen, squeezing the breath out of the chests of the men. Never will forget that, no way."

Glenn snapped open a leather sheath he always wore on his belt and took out his hunting knife. He began to pare a broken thumbnail with the big, shiny blade.

"Everything was going smooth," he said, peering intently at the nail. "The road up the mountain was kind of narrow for that interstate, she was a wide sucker, I had to back her up and take a couple runs at some of the hairpins and I'm jus' coming 'round one about five, six miles an hour and boom! I'm face-to-face with a Mill Valley cop and there ain't enough room either side for him to get by. I do think he was a little taken by surprise to see that big ole bus with Reno on the front. Right?

"I explained the whole mixup to him, how the bus was sitting there and all, and that I planned to return it to them in the morning and all. Heck, the clutch pedal was loose and I even had it in my mind to tighten it down if this lady had any tools up at her place. I was naked and that went against me some, but it was so damn warm and when I went past San Quentin and all I soaked myself sweating.

"Then once I was in Napa and everything I had to see this

psychologist every week. I just kind of toyed with his mind, played mind games, but one day he says to me, 'Glenn, you can jerk my string every week for the rest of your goddamn life and learn nothing, or you can try to level with yourself and maybe figure out what got you here.'

"I heard that," Glenn said, "I really did. He was right, you know? So I did it like he said, I leveled with him and started in talking about stuff I'd never said outloud. I *was* only nineteen.

"Larry Seligman, I got to really looking forward to talking to him, I felt like I was finally getting my mind in order, like. Larry was good people, real good people. Then one Tuesday I showed up at three-thirty like always and Larry wasn't there in his office. I go in there and there's this other guy and he says Larry's been transferred and he's taking over for him.

"I'm thinking fast, I mean I'm sitting there asking myself should I trust this guy? Who is he anyway? Can I just keep on like it was Larry there? But I got to, don't I? So I say, okay, and I start in talking and in a little bit this guy cuts in. 'Mr. Hittel, *Mister* Hittel!'

" 'Mister Hittel, Seligman is gone I told you. The time for jiving and bullshit is over.' "

Glenn resheathed the hunting knife and held up his thumb to examine his handiwork in the light. I was relieved when he put his knife away. I wasn't accustomed to a man trimming his nails with a blade the size of a hero sandwich, and it gave his tale a frightening edge.

Paul said, "You didn't tell me this part before. Christ, what did you do?"

"I leaned across the desk and hit the dumb sumbitch in the mouth," Glenn said, "Right? He hit the panic button and started screaming and all and they came running and tied me up in a strait-jacket. I didn't see as how I had a choice, not really, because if I didn't hit him I'd lose everything I learned talking to Larry like that. I was gettin' out of there one way or another, only it was going to take a tad longer than I thought."

* * *

161

The jug was empty and the beer was gone too. Lil and Sue had dropped Estelle around and split again. Glenn was going to spend the night. Estelle was down in Paul's bedroom, and we threw pads and sleeping bags down on the upstairs floor, using the cushions from the sofa for pillows.

"I'm gonna take a look up at my stompin' grounds tomorrow," Glenn said. "It's a funny thing, I'm kind of like a rat scurrying around the same small area. I just love Pine Ridge, Spiller Canyon, Cathedral Creek Divide, and stuff. It's just a little piece of the wilderness but it can just about take up all your time. Hey, Paul, you want to come up there?"

Paul turned over in his bag and propped his chin on a bent elbow. "I've got work to do, I'm beginning my book again. Ben may want to go, though."

"You're real welcome," Glenn said. "I'm takin' off right when I wake up."

Rising early had very little appeal, nor did taking off with Glenn. His story had had such an elemental intensity that I found myself wary of him. I had wanted to ask him to put his knife away, but couldn't. But I still wanted to talk to him about who Rich Hanna's partner might have been, so I put aside my reluctance.

"Sure," I said. "Thanks." I told myself that an early start would be just the remedy for the wine-filled night.

"You know what I meant to ask you more about, Glenn?" Paul said after he snapped off the last lamp and the room was plunged into sudden darkness. "Did that arson guy say how they were able to tell it was probably set, and what prevented them from being certain?"

"Oh, they got ways of tracking a fire right back to where it started, following the burn, I guess that wouldn't be too difficult. And it was a campground, so that makes it more'n likely some person started it. But, you know, it ain't so remote as when Sue and I camped there, they got a dirt track now and power lines 'n' all, so it just might have been an accident, that's the five percent of doubt, people coming by."

I was dozing off. I already knew that the fire at Lost Valley was arson, and that nature had cooperated by spitting lightning from a frustrated storm into the parched slope of Uncle Sam thirty-six hours later. What was interesting in what Glenn was saying was that this arsonist had not sent a message, as most arsonists will. One way or another a person who sets fires almost always wants it known the fire was set, otherwise his message isn't delivered, his satisfaction incomplete. But the person who set the Lost Sam blaze didn't want it known.

Which only made it more evident who had torched the wilderness, and why.

Twenty-Eight

It was silent out there on Pine Ridge the way only the wilderness can be. In the damp, smokey dawn nothing stirred, no birds announced the arrival of a new day, no leaves swayed in the light morning breeze. What had recently been Valley Oaks were now black, craggy skeletons. The few remaining leaves were also black, or a dark oily brown. Glenn and I looked out over a valley of ash.

I was still thickheaded with sleep, my mind trailing whispers of the night that had passed too fast; it seemed like the moment I fell into a swarming and ungraspable dream I had started awake with Glenn shaking my shoulder. We had pulled on our clothes in the grayish dark and begun the slow drive up here to Pine Ridge. Several times as we bumped along my neck snapped and I came awake with a start, realizing I had slipped back into sleep's refuge again.

We left the van and walked to the ridge through an aisle of black, stalagmite-shaped tree trunks, our steps raising little clouds of powdery ash.

I was limping pretty badly, my twisted ankle playing up in the cold morning air.

"How's the ankle?" Glenn asked.

"It'll do," I said, and limped after him until he reached the ridge.

"Judas H. Cricket," Glenn said, his eyes sweeping the devastation the Lost Sam fire had visited on his wilderness. "Nothing made it through up in here, I have never seen anything like this before. It's like Roy says, once you've seen it burned clean you'll know it in a whole different way. It's naked, I never have seen it naked before."

The revelation of the earth's hidden contours was deeply sensuous, the ash drawn into long, soft curves like the sand in the desert. For an instant I felt as if I were seeing it through Glenn's eyes. There was something disturbingly magnetic about Glenn, I had felt it last night when he told the story about the school bus, and I felt it again now.

He knelt in the ash and unsnapped the clasp on his knife sheath. He withdrew his hunting knife. The curved blade edge gleamed when he slid the point into the ash. It seemed as though the ash accepted the blade, neither parting nor resisting, simply making room for it.

" 'Bout one and three-quarter, two inches deep," Glenn said, sliding the knife free and assessing the depth of ash collected on the blade.

I was watching him wipe the blade clean on the ankle of his jeans when an orange ant hurried across the top of his dusty work boots and onto his thick white sock.

"Look," I said, "he made it."

"Who? Oh, him," Glenn said. "Yep, must of been down deep in his hole." He stood upright and looked off toward the horizon, his eyes tracing the valley. Curls of smoke from smoldering hot spots rose from the ash, some of the blackened trunks hissed. "It's all going to come back like new," he said, nodding. "Man, this is a real eye-opener." Somewhere in the distance I heard but did not see a charred tree give up the ghost and fall to earth.

Glenn yelped suddenly, and swatted at his sock. Then he knelt and picked the orange ant off the sock on a spatulated finger. "Hey, you guys bite," he said, crushing the ant under his thumb.

As he ended the life of that tiny, annoying survivor with all the majestic indifference of a god, or a fire, to what it is destroying, I understood at last. It had all been obvious and I didn't know why it had taken me so long to put it together into a coherent story. Glenn's lying about even smoking dope; the failure of his "trust" to pay up on time this year; what Dink had told me about Rich Hanna's partner trouble; what had been revealed in Rich's bank statement. Even the import of the story Glenn had told last night. I was trying to decide how to handle this disturbing knowledge, what to do about it, when Glenn said, "You know, I had a real good time last night. What I like about Paul is his sincerity."

"You're no goddamn friend of Paul's," I said heatedly, stung by the false sentiment at just that moment. And then immediately regretted what I had done. Glenn reacted as if I had slapped him, drawing up and looking at me with undisguised shrewdness.

"You got it all figured out, don't you?" Glenn said. He shook his head violently, as if to clear it. I couldn't rip my eyes away from the hunting knife still held loosely in his big red fist at the end of his long arm. "But I don't think you really understand why."

Softly as I could I said, "Tell me, Glenn."

"Rich and me, we were partners," he said. "I found out he was stealing from my end. Stealing my money. I mean, he always kept more than a fair share, for the risks he took he said. But this year he was taking too long paying me what I was owed. He was giving me some booshwah story that he thought maybe somebody was watchin' him and he was lookin' after me, keeping me safe from it."

I kept watching Glenn, who seemed to be giving in to some deep-seated desire to talk about what he had done. I sensed I was barely there for him, like the second shrink in his story, the one who had made a wrong response and whom he had hit. He just had to say these things, to get them outside himself. There was nothing either boastful or guilty about Glenn's tone and attitude, just the same indwelling intensity I had seen illuminating him last night.

"I'm down in Brown's Lumber," he continued, as if he could see the scene in front of him, "and Peyton's in there buying three dozen two-penny nails and he tells me Rich is preparing to sell out to him, putting an end to their boundary dispute and all. That's right when I came to my senses, I had my fill of Rich playing me for the fool. I went out looking for him and he was up near Paul's place, on his nine.

"Before I could get all the way up to him, there's Paul coming, holding his ax. They didn't see me watching them, I was some way back in the trees and it was smokey and all. I stood there watching the whole damn thing going down. Paul was grabbing onto his ax like he wanted to kill him, and Rich said something to him, and Paul swung the ax blade into the old oak and ran off. Couldn't do it.

"Rich is laughing like at Paul, so I come up to him then. He says, 'Didja see the little pansy run home?'

"I say, 'Rich, Peyton told me you're planning to sell out to him. You planning on taking my money along with you too when you leave this place?' He kind of smiled, sarcasticlike. I had him caught out.

"I yanked Paul's ax out of that oak and finished the job for him, that's all."

Glenn's bulging eyes slowly refocused as he came fully back to where we stood on the ash ridge.

"I *am* Paul's friend," he said. "I got a plan. What I was going to do was get the hell out of here, make myself scarce. There's nothing keeping me any longer, me 'n' Sue, our time's past, we ain't got kids or nothing. I was all set to go, but this fire, you know. I had to see it to the end. What I was going to do as soon as I could, I was going to write a letter telling them that I was the one who killed Rich Hanna, so they would know Paul's innocent. I couldn't go to jail, I couldn't breathe in there."

I could almost see Glenn's mind working over the problem

167

of what to do about me, now that I knew. Before he had a chance to draw the inevitable conclusion, I threw myself at his knees, and we went down in a tumble. As we hit the ground I felt my bad ankle buckle and snap under me, and a blinding pain. I was grasping desperately for Glenn's knife hand, but he wriggled free somehow, jumping up and dancing away from me. The fear was strong in my gut.

"I don't want to hurt you, man," he shouted. "I ain't like that. Stop!"

I lunged for him again, but my leg wouldn't support my weight and I went down in a heap. I tried to crawl after him on all fours, but he backed away faster than I could follow. I was on my hands and knees looking up at the knife in his hand. He stopped well out of my reach and looked at the knife himself. Then he slid it back into the empty sheath.

"Your leg's broke," he said. "The bone's poking right through." And then in the same tone of voice he added, "I'm not going to hurt you." He shook his head violently again, as if to clear it.

"Fair enough, man, okay?" he said. "Fair enough." He turned and went back to his van and drove away.

The sun was up, a bright yellow disc visible through the lifting haze. I tried to get to my feet and collapsed again. I didn't have the goddamnest idea what to do now.

Twenty-Nine

All I could do was hobble down the track toward the road and hope somebody would come along. I looked for a branch to use as a crutch, but all the fallen wood was burned down to ash. The pain in my ankle was excruciating, I couldn't put any weight on it at all and had to hop, catching hold of an outcrop of rock when I could. Several times I pitched forward onto all fours; the ground was rough and uneven and the way down was steep.

I had gone maybe a quarter of a mile in the time it took for the sun to move from the horizon to a point above the eastern timberline when I heard a vehicle approaching, way before I saw it. I thought: Glenn's coming back, he's realized that he had better kill me after all.

I knew that in order to survive I would have to kill him. I looked around for a big stone that would fit into my hand. My readiness to kill Glenn if I could came as a kind of revelation. It was an awesome force inside of me, vast and deep and irresistible. Beside it free will seemed a feather in a tornado.

I grasped hold of a pretty-good-size gray stone, rounded on one side and rough on the other. It was still cold with the night. I hauled myself up on my knees, because I had the firmest base when I was kneeling. I put as much weight as I could on my left hand, leaving my stone-holding hand free. The pain in my ankle came in waves and when they crested it went black behind my eyes. I was drenched in sweat. To have completely favored the ankle, I would have had to leave myself badly unbalanced.

Glenn's van drew closer and closer. It came over the top of the hill. I realized belatedly that he could just leave the road and run me over. So I began to crawl up the embankment toward an outcropping of rocks that would block the way of the van. It seemed impossibly far away, too far to reach in the time I had. I glanced back over my shoulder to see how close he was now, panting, and saw instead Lil opening the door of Paul's red Bronco and running toward me. I flopped over onto my back, my chest heaving.

"Holy cow," I said out loud, letting my breath out in a violent release of tension. I was saved. That bed of ash and earth was suddenly the softest place I had ever lain.

"Are you okay? My God, he didn't kill you?" Lil cried. "You're covered in ash, you look like a ghost. Oh God," she cried, and threw her arms around my neck.

Paul ran up with a rifle in his hands.

"What happened?" he barked, "Where is he?"

How in God's name did they know that Glenn might have tried to harm me?

"You okay?" Paul repeated.

"Broken ankle is all, I think. Listen, quick," I said, "there's time once we start driving to talk, let's just get in the car and head after him. Wait a minute," I said, immediately contradicting myself, "Didn't you pass Glenn on his way down when you were coming up here?"

They both shook their heads no, they hadn't.

"He must have taken the track over into Railly Canyon," Lil said. "That's another one of his haunts."

"Wouldn't he just make a run for the county road?" I asked. "Get as far away as he could as fast as he could go?"

"That makes sense," Paul said.

"Here, Paul," Lil said, holding me under one arm. "Get on his other side, we'll support him."

We made it down to the car that way and as soon as we started driving down back toward Scottsburg I said to Paul, "How did you know?"

"Lil did," he said.

I looked at her questioningly.

"Yesterday, before the funeral, I asked Glenn if he had any ideas about who Rich's silent partner could be, and I could see the question took him aback. He said he had no idea, didn't even know Rich had a partner. I made a mistake then," Lil said, "I told him we had heard Rich had some partner trouble.

"Glenn asked me where I heard that and I saw, maybe I was saying too much, and that kind of alerted me. I mean, Glenn and Sue are real close friends and why should I all of a sudden feel funny about telling him this stuff? So I just said, 'Up in San Francisco,' you know.

"But I knew he was lying as soon as he said to me he didn't know Rich had a partner. I blurted out that stuff about partner trouble. It was real, real weak of me." She put her hand on mine and squeezed, and I squeezed back.

"Okay," I said. "But why didn't you say something to me about it yesterday, if you were suspicious?"

"When? You and I never had a chance to talk alone. I told you, remember, that I had something I wanted to tell you? But Glenn was right there. And he was still there with you when Sue and I dropped Estelle back around.

"And I wasn't entirely sure of myself either. I had plenty of time to doubt it. I had called Dink, you see? I went into Glenn and Sue's while they were out and I found some tax returns and got Glenn's social security number. And I called Dink. I found his card in my bag ripped in two."

"He was glad to hear from you?"

She shot me a warning look. "Ecstatic, and anxious to do me a favor. I explained exactly what I needed to know, and why, and how it was urgent. He called back about six o'clock this morning, called Paul. I don't know how he got Paul's number now that I think of it but he had some way, and he told Paul why he was calling and what he had found. And Paul came rushing down and got me, you and Glenn were already gone up to Pine Ridge. I gave Paul one of Glenn's rifles and we came up here after you."

"What did Dink find out exactly?" I asked.

"Oh, that Glenn made a deposit, a big deposit, every year a few days after Rich, never as much as Rich's and the difference was getting bigger every year. And this year Rich deposited sixty-five thousand dollars three weeks ago and Glenn's account was in overdraft. *That's* why he was having trouble making his mortgage."

"It was all pretty clear by then," Paul said. "But what happened up there?"

"Men, goddammit, I swear," Lil said. Her beautiful face was dusted in white ash, like a clown's and there were streaks down her cheeks where tears had dried.

"What?" Paul and I said simultaneously. "What?"

"You," she told me. "*You* asked *him* how *he* figured it out."

Thirty

The surprises weren't over with.

While Paul drove I told them how I had suddenly come to understand up on Pine Ridge that Glenn had murdered Rich. By the time I finished my abbreviated version of the falling out between partners, we were almost in Scottsburg, all hundred triangular feet of it.

There in the road around the rural route mailboxes, like a bunch of your friends and relations jumping out from behind sofas and closet doors on your birthday and shouting, "Surprise!" were Tommy Garber, Sheriff Etter, his green-and-white car and two deputies, Estelle, Roy Hanna, Annie Bayard, and trussed up on a gurney with a white blood-stained bandage around his head and his straw hat with its rakish feather resting on his chest, Glenn.

There were other people too, drawn by the Sheriff and the ambulance, but I didn't notice who.

"I'll be damned," Paul said, slowing down. Young Tommy provided the first explanation. As we piled out he ran over and rubbed against Lil like a cat, except without that feline guile.

"I, I, I . . ." he stuttered. And then: "Is Glenn hurt bad, Lil? They said he got a concushion in his head," making it sound like a couch cushion.

She put her arm around his trembling shoulders. "How'd this happen, Tommy?" she asked gently.

As I hobbled out of the Bronco, Estelle rushed up and took hold of my arm, I lost my balance and fell into her, and we both stumbled in each other's arms before righting ourselves against the front fender.

"He hurt you," she said.

"No, I'm okay, it's just an ankle." I patted her back to reassure her. "But what's going on, how did you get down here with all these people?"

"Me? Oh, the Sheriff came around looking for Lil or you and then he drove me back down here because I didn't want to stay alone with that killer loose."

"Good, good," I said absently, really more interested in what Tommy was telling Lil. And what Etter was talking about with Paul and Annie Bayard.

Tommy was saying: ". . . when he come all the way up 'n' started in taking that tarp off, I jumped down off'n the rock because I could see it was only Glenn 'n' all. That hunting knife he pulled when he heard me scared me so bad and I din't mean to hurt him, Lil, I din't, really not. I only sort of swung my ax handle 'cause I was so scared, and Glenn started bleeding and all . . ."

Tommy's stakeout in Railly Canyon. I had forgotten all about it. It had been Glenn's getaway gear.

Meanwhile Sheriff Etter was saying to Paul: ". . . then after Miz Palmer's call, Tommy here was riding up to his Uncle Roy's with Glenn Hittel bleeding and woozy back in the bed of the pickup just about when we were arriving to see what in hell all this was supposed to be about. Henry!" he said when he noticed I was listening. "You tell me what's going on here without any American Civil Liberties horseshit." Then to Estelle, " 'Scuse my language, m'am."

About midway through my narrative one of the ambulance

174

attendants interrupted. "Sheriff, this man should be in ER, is that okay?"

"What?" said Etter. "Sure, you boys shove off. My deputy'll ride with Hittel."

Glenn suddenly sat up as far as his restraints allowed, about thirty degrees. "Paul!" he shouted.

Everybody turned to face him. "Hey, good buddy," Glenn said. "Don't forget 'n' return that Winchester you got there, my daddy gave that rifle to me." He smiled as if he had told an awfully good joke and pitied us all for not getting it. Then he lay his head down and closed his eyes. They wheeled him onto the ambulance and took him away.

Finally, I laughed. I laughed and laughed and laughed from deep down in my diaphragm because I was alive. I couldn't even hate Glenn, who after all might have killed me but didn't. He was a psychological mess, and he was wicked, but I didn't think he was evil. He would be out in a couple of years bearing no grudges and surprised to be borne any ill will for what he had done.

My ankle was throbbing and I really wanted to sit down and rest it, so I let myself down right there in the road as gingerly as I could.

Tommy came close to me and squatted on his haunches, looking anxious.

"I'm okay, Tom, I really am."

He was rocking back and forth with his arms wrapped around his drawn-up knees, and I realized it wasn't my injury that was concerning him.

"I'm real condolences, Mr. Henry, real condolences," he said bravely, fighting back his tears.

"Real condolences? I don't—oh, condolences, sorry. What are you sorry about, Tom?"

"Hurtin' Glenn, I'm scared he's going to die too like grandma and Rich," he said, and started to bawl.

I leaned closer and put my arm around his back. "Glenn's going to be okay, Tom, you gave him a bump, that's all."

"Boy," said Roy Hanna, who had come over and squatted

beside his grandson, "what you did was brave, you've got nothing to be ashamed of."

"You captured him, Tom," I said. "Glenn was the suspicious gangster."

"Glenn? I . . . ?"

"Looks like it was Glenn who killed your uncle Rich, Tommy," said Roy Hanna. "That gear up in Railly Canyon was his survival kit, he was fixing on gettin' away until you put a stop to that damn nonsense." The man had buried his wife not twenty-four hours before.

Across Roy's bent back as he talked to the boy my eyes locked with Annie Bayard's. The look we exchanged and held was as naked as the valley of ash, as remorseless as death.

Thirty-One

"Think of it as an interrupted conversation," Lil said to me on the morning that I left Scottsburg. She kissed me softly on my lips, then she got into her battered little Toyota and drove away from Paul's house without looking back or waving.

She was right, it did feel like an interruption. Which made my second interrupted conversation in a year. First Jessica, now Lil. I didn't know if Jessica would return, or if she did, what would have changed between us. But Lil was here now, and that was more than good enough. While I had rested and let my ankle grow accustomed to its cast, we had talked and talked; the talk was interspersed with times when if we were not exactly quiet then at least we were mostly wordless. But as each day passed it became clearer and clearer that my ankle was only an excuse for staying on. It was time to go back to San Francisco.

One of the things we had talked about, naturally, was Annie Bayard's involvement in Eve Hanna's death. Paul and Lil and Estelle and I had talked about it all together, and in different combinations. By the time Paul took Estelle to San Francisco airport on Friday, nothing was resolved. Estelle was primarily

177

relieved that we hadn't acted, she didn't want to see us in-volved in any more trouble. Paul, meanwhile, couldn't make his mind up; he'd still be turning it this way and that long after the time to act had passed. In the end he'd have thought about it more deeply than the rest of us, and learned the most along the way. Lil had made up her mind there was no obligation on her to intervene in the most private affairs of the Hanna family. As for me, I knew I had to do something but didn't know what.

After Lil drove off Paul ambled out of the house with a steaming mug of coffee in his hand and no shoes or shirt on.

"How'd you get service?" I asked him.

"Management never mentions it has the right not to refuse service to anyone too," he said. "Bunko, listen, there's some-thing I want to tell you. I've been doing a lot of thinking, I suppose we all have. I've decided, I'm going back to live in Chicago. What I think is, if I can write this book I can do it as easily in Chicago as here, more easily maybe. And Estelle, well, you and I are the only family she's got and she isn't getting any younger. I'll have my own place and all, but I can kind of keep an eye on her."

And his mother an eye on him, I thought. I said, "Thus ends what your biographers will undoubtedly come to see as the Natty Bumpo period in your life."

"And I want to pay you."

"Pay me, Paulie?" I screeched, feeling blood rush to my face.

"I've been giving what you did for me, and how to show my thanks, a lot of thought too. So when I took Estelle up to the airport I took a detour—here." He held out an envelope.

I nixed the transaction with my hands, like warding off a hex, as I backed away from the envelope. "No way, Paulie, I don't want it."

He insisted. "Look ingodamnside, will you for crying out loud."

Reluctantly, like Adam taking a bite of the apple, and fear-ful of many of the same consequences, I took the envelope from his outstretched hand. It wasn't sealed and I opened the flap. Inside was a receipt for two season tickets to the Giants. The box was in section 4, which Paulie knew was on the third-base line where I liked to sit. The flimsy sheet of pink paper spoke volumes to me about love and friendship.

I laughed with embarrassment at how moved I was and tried to think of some way to respond. "Damn, you know, Paulie— sorry," I said, coughing to clear my throat. "That's better. What set Glenn off up there, Pine Ridge, was he said he liked you and I said no, he wasn't your friend. I said it really vehemently, and I've been thinking about it, just what I meant, you know? Because Glenn came when you needed help, I mean he looked after your place when the fire was closing in and you were in jail. And that's what most of us would say friendship is, right, someone who'll come help in the middle of the night? And he was going to write that letter to let you off.

"But Glenn was willing to screw you really badly to save himself. Deep down, isn't a friend someone you know won't ever harm you? That's how I feel about you, and I think it's a damn sight rarer than someone who'll show up in the middle of the night."

We hugged.

I found Tommy at the Hanna trailer the way I hoped to.

"Everybody's gone off," he said. "Uncle Roy's gone to King City."

"Well, it was you I was really looking for," I told him. "I've got to be getting back home."

"You goin' to Frisco, Mr. Henry?"

"I am."

"Can I ride with you out to the county road? I can walk back, no problem."

"Hop in," I said.

"Boy, this is really a neat car," Tommy said.

"Thanks. I almost got a red one, you think that would have been better?"

"Nah, I like this one the best, black."

"You like San Francisco, Tom?"

"I don't know, I never been. Furthest I ever went myself was to San Jose that time for Annie when she said I had to go bring grandma some medicine."

San Jose was a long way to go for medicine. "Annie had you go to San Jose especially?"

"The doctors wasn't giving her the medicine she most needed so grandpa and Annie tole me special to go see this one fella, this doctor he was, at a place Annie used to work up there. He gave grandma what she needed. Annie wrote down the directions and his name and the name of the medicine and a map 'n' all," he said proudly.

"Annie told you not to tell anybody about it, didn't she, Tom?"

He instantly looked sheepish.

"It's okay to discuss it with me, Tommy, because I'm a private eye and have to know some things. You remember what the medicine was called?"

"No," he shook his head. We were nearly at the county road. I rolled onto the gravel shoulder and set the brake.

"Listen, Tom, how about you come up to see me in San Francisco sometime soon? We can go to a Giants game, how does that sound?"

"Really? No kidding?" He tore off his hat and whapped it across his knees. "Yahoo!" Then he jumped out of the car and slammed the door.

I waved and pulled slowly back toward the road, the gravel crunching beneath my tires.

"Mr. Henry!" Tommy shouted, running after the car. "Wait! I remember! It was like succotash or something."

I braked. "Succinylcholine?"

"That's it!"

Though as the crow flies it was only a few miles distant from Lost Sam's burn, the pastureland along the bank of the Car-

mel River was green and wet and lush. I shut off the motor and
the silence rushed in. The only inhabitants of the stretch of
pasture where I was stopped were willow trees, phone lines,
a rough-hewn fence strung with two strands of wire, and
orange signs nailed to the fence posts. The signs were the
noisiest things in the pasture, noisier than the magpie: POSTED,
they shouted.

Every few minutes another car sped by on the G16. I could
hear it coming a long way off, its motor growing more and
more distinct until it ripped past and out of sight, trailing the
whispering of its wheels along the tarmac like a mile-long tail.
A truck passed, its load banging around in the flatbed. Somewhere back in the black-green hillside across the river a bird
honked.

The sun was sinking behind the dark lumps of hillside.
What was it about men and sunsets? Lil had asked, and I had
said sunsets bored me. But when you are alone and there are
unfinished matters on your mind and in your heart, sunset is
a powerful time, dense with faith and anxiety.

What young Tommy had told me amounted to just this:
Roy and Annie had killed Eve. If I were to trust the judicial
process to decide on the criminality of what they had done, I
would also be opening Eve Hanna up to posthumous judicial
scrutiny. And that was something I could not do. I had blun-
dered into their world at their time of reckoning to help my
friend, who had failed ultimately to make a home among these
people. Really neither Paul nor I had been much more than
bystanders as they enacted their drama of destruction and
salvation. Eve had returned home from the laetrile clinic in
Mexico knowing she was dying. That was the day before
someone started a fire in Lost Valley, before Eve had started
the fire. The arson was an act of reckless love. Love for her
husband, who was going to lose her soon anyway but didn't
have to lose his land to taxes and vacation chalets if the
insurance company paid up when the Hanna's big new house
was burned to the ground. And love for the forest that was a

181

third party to their forty-year union. "This Lost Sam is good for the forest," I remembered her saying. "It's going to leave the forest clean and new again. Ain't it, Roy?"

"She did all a woman could do," Roy had said when I offered him my condolences after his wife died. Roy was like a king whose women performed miraculous acts of courage and sacrifice for him.

He had done his duty, too, with the help of Annie Bayard. The Hannas, and Annie Bayard, and even Glenn in his distorted way were all unconfused people. They had no hesitation in deciding for themselves what was right and what wrong. And when they knew, they acted. The fire had been Eve's parting gift to her husband, the succinylcholine his to her. Eve Hanna's death had been of her own choosing, a death as harmonious with the natural order of things as a human being can devise.

Lil and Estelle had been right in their different ways, it was none of our business. Eve was buried now in a dry and thirsty ground but her reckless love, in time, would make it green and fresh anew.